The Stagecoach

A Western Novel

Richard G. Hole

Far West

SYNOPSIS

The Missouri stagecoach consisted of four old vehicles, large, heavy, discolored, but heavily armored,

Two carriages made the outward journey, while the other two made the return journey, which lasted a week.

The name of the line was due to the fact that the cars ran parallel to the Missouri River during half of their trip and the other half traveled through the valley, leaving the river to the left as they advanced towards the divide.

The stagecoach is a story belonging to the Far West collection, a collection of novels developed in the American Wild West.

THE STAGECOACH

CHAPTER I

A BUSINESSMAN

The Missouri Stagecoach, the name by which it was known in the region, was a quartet of old vehicles, large, heavy, discolored, but heavily armored, which made the journey from almost central Nebraska, departing from Dunning, to finish trip in Marsland, to two hundred miles of the starting point and already almost in the limit of the region, to fifty miles by the North of South Dakota and another fifty by the western Wyoming.

Two carriages made the outward trip, while the other two made the return trip, which lasted a week, and the name of the line was due to the fact that the cars ran parallel to the Missouri River during half of their trip and the other half the they traversed the valley, leaving the river to the left as they advanced toward the divide.

Part of the route seemed almost unnecessary to do it following the railway line, which ran the same route to Seneca, but there the railway line descended downwards away from a fairly populated sector and the stagecoach made up for this lack, putting in communication, with the rest of the State, to the towns scattered in this piece of valley.

Further north, at a distance of about twenty miles, another river, the Northern Lupp, ran parallel to the course of the Missouri, but both died in the middle of the line and no longer found waterways until reach the Niobrara, which crossed precisely at Marsland where the stagecoach died.

On Tuesdays and Saturdays at mid-afternoon, as if it were a timed thing, one of the two stagecoaches that went up to the Northwest crossed through Nirvay, and on Mondays and Fridays the ones that descended at the head of the line did.

Nirvay, a town near the railroad and a short distance from the Missouri, was a fairly discreet town, with some brick buildings, such as the City Hall, the Post Office, and the Banco Ganadero and, in general, its houses were clean and attractive. its streets less dusty than those of many towns in the region and its hard-working and industrious inhabitants.

There were two important wood sawmills in the town that provided a good contingent of workers, several well-kept farms that worked cheese, butter and other products, many shops of various kinds, and in the valley part, some important ranches.

The railroad and the river made Nirvay a town with a lot of commercial traffic and, therefore, the Banco Ganadero enjoyed excellent credit and an unusual movement of funds.

The Bank was founded by Alfred Hamson, with two other partners named Smith and Ariliss, who made up the company name for some time, but later, Hamson managed to bypass the partnership, keeping the shares of his colleagues.

And he was the Managing Director and owner, with no other guardianship than a Board of Directors appointed by him among some residents of the town, who met twice a year, approved the complicated accounts that Hamson put before their eyes without understanding anything of them, and later, they would meet to eat with the proprietary Director, spending a happy and happy day and receiving the semiannual allowances that were assigned to them for their little work.

They all had great confidence in Alfred Hamson. He had been a rancher until two years ago, who sold the ranch to a neighbor, retiring to private life to enjoy his well-earned benefits.

Hamson took shelter in a beautiful country house that had been built in the valley, a short distance from the town, and every day, punctually, he would go down to the bank in his gig to take care of his administration, together with the three employees who he had at his command.

He was the one who solved all financial issues, who authorized or denied loans on land, livestock, farms and crops, and who, personally, led the banking movement, while his dependents were relegated to the bureaucratic functions of the business.

But Hamson couldn't settle for such a slow job. It is true that the Bank should render a reasonable profit on its movement, but the money standing in the boxes did not produce logically.

And Hamson speculated with him, studying the stock market, contributing reasonable amounts to the wool and wheat markets, acquiring or selling shares in the railroads, waterfalls, construction companies in the region, and this contribution served to the enlargement of the valley and, at the same time, to increase the Bank's profits, which were his own.

Before selling the ranch, he had been left a widower with a single daughter as heir. Sylvia was a fair-haired girl, of good stature, supple as a palm tree, and graceful of features.

Her father took her to be educated at a Hastings college three years ago, for various reasons that mixed convenience, sentimentality, and the pride of having a daughter who set herself apart in education from the other girls in the locality.

Hamson might not have done so, simply hiring the private services of the village teacher, if several intermingled factors had not forced him to worry about Sylvia more intensely than he usually did.

When the mother of the young woman died, she was eighteen years old, and although she had gone to school learning certain preliminary subjects, her tendencies were not towards display and packaging. He had grown up on the ranch among cowboys and that was a simple life, without complications, which gave him almost absolute freedom when he rode a horse and got lost in the pastures or the landscape, far from all parental control.

This led Sylvia to cultivate in an alarming way, according to her father's criteria, the friendship with Frank Neil, a nice, attractive, unruly and non-judgmental boy, who had become part of the ranch team, because that is how he he had pleaded with Hamson, Ted Neil, the boy's father and owner of one of the major warehouses in Nirvay.

On Sundays Sylvia would go down to the village on horseback, leave her mount in the square and spend the afternoon at the dance, where Frank was waiting eagerly for her, and without worrying about the comments that such friendship could provoke, they monopolized each other dancing all the time. the afternoon incessantly, given over to the happiest of talks. Some Saturday afternoons he would wait for her far from the ranch and both of them, on horseback, would go away into the valley, walking and stopping to have a picnic at the foot of a stream and in the shade of the trees, not returning until the sun began to sink in the line. ravine of the distant mountains.

Frank would discreetly accompany her to the vicinity of the ranch, and then, he would go to the town without this friendship and these interviews being known to Hamson.

But one day someone came to him with the story and Alfred screamed to heaven. He didn't think there was anything between the two of them beyond a simple friendship, but he had to prevent those relationships from taking more flights immediately. He did not stop to judge that Frank was a better or worse boy than others who haunted his daughter. He only took into consideration that she was his daughter, the daughter of a rancher, owner of the Banco Ganadero in the town, and that Frank was only a laborer on his ranch, already much concede, the son of a grocer who owned a good store, but nothing that was in parallel with his lineage and wealth.

Furious, he rebuked Frank for his daring courting his daughter and fired him from the ranch, threatening him with severe reprisals if he found out again that he was dealing with her; and he lectured his daughter beautifully for her little head and dignity in cultivating a friendship unworthy of her position.

Neither of them seemed to give much importance to Alfred's anger, and in secret they saw each other a few times, but Hamson, who had had his daughter watched, discovered the new interviews and decided to cut them off. He sent his daughter to a college in Hastings, making her understand that the daughter of a banker had to have a careful education; and not satisfied with this, he tried to chase Frank to the limit.

Valid of his position, he begged in a way that, more than I pray, was a threat, to all the ranchers and farmers of the surroundings not to facilitate work for Frank, and since it was convenient for all of them to be on good terms with the owner of the Bank, since they had having needed his friendship and his business many times, no one dared to admit him to their estates.

Frank could have taken refuge in the warehouse of his father, who needed his services very much, but the boy had not been born to be a merchant, and bored because he could not find work and desperate because Sylvia had disappeared from the village, one day he rode on horseback and He also disappeared, heading for Hastings, in the mad hope that he might see Sylvia, but the harsh rules of the school, augmented by Hamson's predictions, thwarted his attempt.

Even more desperate for this failure, he left the capital and lost himself to the West, determined to forget and make his own way.

Just gone missing, an unclear event occurred at Hamson's ranch. Several cattle were missing and, according to rumors that the banker had circulated, his men had recognized Frank among the cattlemen.

The rumor, the assertion of one of the ranch laborers and the influence of Hamson, gave signs of truth to the matter, and Frank, not only was questioned, but also exposed to be arrested and judged as a cattle dealer if he returned to town.

Months later he wrote to his father from Nevada. Ted, who had a serious altercation with Hamson due to the accusation against his son, wrote to him giving an account of what happened and begging him to refrain from returning at some time, since the influence of the banker could lead him to jail.

Frank answered his father very laconically. He told her in the letter that Sylvia was not there, she had no interest in going back, but that if one day she decided to do so, she would take Hamson by the neck and be twisting him until he confessed that the theft of the cattle was an affair. slander.

Ted freaked out. He knew his son well; He tasted good, hard-working and decent, but he also tasted impulsive and rapturous when he lost control of his nerves and he did not doubt that this threat would be carried out without stopping to ponder the consequences.

But time was passing.

Hamson was at ease without Sylvia, who was not hindering his movements, and for three years he limited himself to making a few trips to Hastings to pay a complimenting visit to his daughter and return to his bank.

Until on her last trip she suffered a terrible disgust when she was told by Sylvia that she considered herself quite educated for a town like Nirvay and that when the vacation came she would return to the town so as not to return to school.

Hamson had to agree. Sylvia was really a full-fledged woman and a financial combination was entering into the calculations of the banker, in which Dennis Powell, son of a wealthy rancher, account holder in his bank and a man who could be ideal for him, was going to play an important role. certain large businesses that he was plotting.

Hamson agreed. Sylvia returned to the village and everyone found her unfamiliar.

She had grown a little, was more stylized and prettier, and her airs were now of an elegance that made the other girls in Nirvay envy.

Sylvia was the first surprised by her own change, because when she saw herself again in her hometown, she observed how the other young women stood out from her in the lower sense and the boys all seemed more uncouth, more ordinary and less deserving of her friendship. and I try.

Frank must have been erased from his memory, or at least he made no allusion to him, and forgetting his old camaraderie and simplicity, he separated himself from commoner parties, from vulgar friendships and had to reduce himself to alternating in the meetings of the judge, the mayor or the notary and attend the dance that the City Council celebrated on the occasion of the Independence party,

When she passed her father's old pawns, when she passed them on horseback, she haughtily greeted them with a slight bow of the head and, little by little, the whole circle of friendships and affections that she had when she left was erased in her new life.

This made him bored in a resounding way. Their diversions were a visit to the town, to the three or four dwellings of the most conspicuous characters of the town, to take great horseback rides and to attend one of the various rodeos that were held in the valley.

Hamson observed this change in his daughter with pleasure, as well as discovered her expression of boredom and boredom, and estimating that the environment was conducive to his plans, he gave Dennis belligerence, inviting him several times to eat and sometimes to a Sunday fishing party in Missouri.

Dennis was a handsome boy, he couldn't be denied. Tall and well-built, he worked little, because his father had entrusted him only with the farm books without allowing him to perform crude and manual functions in it, and this meant that his hands were well cared for, that his skin did not appear tanned by the sun. and the air and that he could dress daily with more elegance than the rest of his neighbors.

Hamson hinted to Sylvia how convenient a possible union of them would be for both families and the young woman, perhaps convinced of such a reason, perhaps out of boredom, perhaps because of forgetting almost dead memories in that regard, or possibly due to family indifference and obedience, did not put it. any obstacle to a possible courtship. And this one arrived meek and cold. One day Dennis, who was also bullied by his father by making him see the good game that Sylvia meant, proposed to her and she accepted as the one who accepts an invitation to a rodeo.

Young Dennis's vanity was filled with acceptance. From that moment on he would be considered the most important young man in the town, overshadowing the loud-mouthed sons of neighboring ranchers, who, because their parents had a good business, considered themselves privileged men in Nirvay.

He, in addition to taking the most beautiful girl, the best educated and of the highest position in the town, threatened to convert this wedding into the most important man in the region, because his father-in-law, sooner or later, would retire from the active life of business by appointing him Managing Director of the Bank, which was as much as putting all the industrialists and merchants within a hundred miles around in his hands and feet.

Hamson was not concerned with the vanity of his future son-in-law or even with his delusional aspirations. His projects were more grandiose and encompassed unsuspected limits and if Dennis dreamed of supplanting him in office and seizing that all-embracing authority that he possessed, he was going to have to wait many years; as many as Hamson had left to live.

For him, his daughter's wedding was a stock market move. If she was pleased and happy, so much the better, and if not ... She would be consoled for failure. There were many ways to resolve that matter later if it arose, but when he had carried out the great deals that he planned and that would not lead him to take advantage of the mayor's office of Nirvay, which is despicable for him, but they would make him a deputy or senator for the State .

CHAPTER II

TEN MINUTES DELAY

That Saturday; Against his custom, since he never went to his office at the Bank on Saturday afternoons, Hamson spent the whole day there. He had had a frugal meal served from a town tavern and alone, without any help from an employee, had been indulged in certain manipulations of great significance for the business.

The Missouri stagecoach would arrive around four o'clock, and an hour later, when it picked up the mail and the few travelers who left the town on Saturday afternoon, it would continue north-west and in which it had to send a bulky sack that it had handled without anyone intervening in the operation.

When the stagecoach arrived and delivered the sack, he had everything prepared to leave Nirvay and although his daughter had asked him to take him with her, he flatly refused, claiming that he was going to secretly deal with a matter of great commercial importance and that the person he was dealing with did not want it to be known that they were in negotiations, in case someone suspected the reason and got ahead of them.

"It's something big, Sylvia," he assured, "something that will round out my position and yours. The day that the people of the valley and even beyond, know it, not only are they going to be astonished, but some are going to pull their hair out when they see that I, more modest than them, have taken a huge business from them. wingspan.

And without wanting to add more, he highly recommended to his daughter that she spend a good Sunday with Dennis and went to the bank where she stayed until just before four o'clock.

At that hour he had in order a voluminous sack of thick leather that weighed quite a bit. It had been tied with a strong wire, the ends caught with a lead that had been crushed as a seal, and then a huge wax seal with its interlocking initials served as a double guarantee that it could not be opened with impunity.

He left it in his locked office, and, crossing the square, he went to the Casa de Postas, which in turn was a post office.

The chief saluted him slavishly and Hamson, beckoning him, whispered in his ear:

"I have to speak to you, Mr. Caster.

The latter offered him his office, and now, the two of them alone, the banker asked:

"Is the foreman of the stagecoach that will arrive in a few minutes trustworthy?

"Very much, Mr. Hamson. It's about old Jasper. He has been doing the tour for seven years and there has never been the slightest complaint about him. Don't you know him?

"By sight, but I have no reports, and I am happy with the reports you provide. So, do you think you can be trusted with anything?

"Without fear of any kind.

"Well. I have to make a risky shipment and there is no other solution than to trust him. A leather sack containing fifty thousand dollars has to come out of here today. It is a transfer that I must make to the Marsland Livestock Bank, without delay. Said Bank has paid that amount on my orders to some ranchers there, trusting in my solvency and I have solemnly promised that the money would come out of here in today's stagecoach. If this were not the case, my credit would be compromised and you will be in charge of what this means for a banking business of the importance of mine.

"Of course I'm in charge," said the boss, "but I don't think there is any objection to his leaving. I will talk to Jasper and let him know the importance of the content, without giving him a figure of what it contains. It is not for nothing, but recommending that the content is valuable will suffice.

"Very well. I have to entrust myself to him, but I don't want this to transcend. The place is not dangerous, there have been few cases of robberies around here, but the line is long, there are favorable places and I am not calm. I suppose that in the stage there will be a suitable place to hide the sack in plain sight.

"Yes. Jasper's seat is hollow. The lid is lifted and inside, under it, it will be hidden.

"Magnificent... Now... the question of travelers. Do many go out on the stage?

"Not today. As you know, on Saturdays and Sundays this is very lively and people instead of leaving here, come. I have only dispatched three tickets. An elderly woman will leave, who goes to Rita Park to meet a niece who is getting married, the daughter of a farmer from the valley, who will get off before reaching the first town near the farm, where she works, and a young woman who goes to Seneca . That's all.

"It's a shame that a cowboy isn't traveling too. A man with a revolver on his belt is a guarantee if something happens on the road.

"What's going to happen, Mr. Hamson? "I don't know, but you will understand that when you have to randomly trust such an amount, you are not at ease until you know it at your destination. Do you realize what such a blow would mean to me and to all my clients? It makes my hair stand on end thinking about it.

"I understand.

"If there was at least a railroad to Marsland, I'd be more at ease. A train is not so easily robbed and the mail car is safer. It is cared for by armed men who would know how to defend it by shooting; but a stagecoach is much worse ... On the other hand, I do not even have the consolation of being able to go in person guarding the bag. Not that I create a hero.

"I haven't exercised with a colt in my hand in a long time, and my years have spoiled my pulse. The pen has defeated the weapons, but I still consider myself with arrests to defend what is entrusted to me until I die with a revolver in my hand.

«I would have done it if the shipment was not so urgent, but there are eight days of travel between roundtrip, eight days that I cannot leave the Bank and, on the other hand, as soon as I deliver the bag, I have to go to celebrate a important interview with a certain character.

«Something big, Mr. Caster! Something that when the result is known, the entire valley will tremble with excitement and rejoicing! I am like that, my friend, I work for myself and for the locality and one day my neighbors will realize exactly the sacrifices that I am making for the town and for the entire valley. I am not selfish, I realize the many needs of the region and I want to be a father to all. If they want to acknowledge it sooner or later, fine, and if not ... I will retire hurt, but with the satisfaction of having fulfilled a duty of citizenship.

"Oh sure!" Replied the chief. You have done a lot for everyone. The founding of the Bank was a success. You do not have to keep money at home with exposure, or send it with exposure outside. On the other hand, you help people in need, you lend them money on livestock, wool, crops, land ... of course with your interests, but what about the favor you do them with it?

"That is what I want you to recognize. Of course I charge interests, and some high ones, and that I demand solid guarantees, and even sometimes I have been forced to execute repossessions, but my friend, I do it with great pain in my heart, because that money is not mine, it is yours , those who have it deposited in my Bank with my guarantee of an honest man. If not, how could I guarantee it and give a modest interest on the deposit? This is clear, even if those affected do not understand it.

Suddenly he cut off his spiel and examined his watch, initiating a movement of impatience:

"Devil!" He muttered. A quarter past four and the stagecoach not arriving! This is another setback. It always arrives rather in advance and today that I have the minutes rated it is delayed. Is bad luck!

"It can't be long now, Mr. Hamson. It is only a quarter of an hour that is delayed ... Any breakdown ...

"But it's a bummer, friend Caster, I have to get out of here immediately ...

He left the office and went out into the square. To the right, the dusty path of the road was clear of all vehicles.

Hamson paced through the door of the Post Office with his hands behind his back, striding and staring continuously at the road, until at last a cloud of dust rose in the distance.

"That must be it," he murmured. He's forty minutes late.

Finally, amidst the dust that blurred the heavy carriage and the jingle of bells that vibrated Argentina, the vehicle appeared. The dusty and sweaty horses advanced to the Post Office, stopping before it without anyone having the need to force them to do so.

The mayoral, a fifty-five-year-old man with unruly gray hair, who was escaping under the brims of his hat, jumped down heavily and opened the door for the seven travelers he was carrying to get out of the carriage. There they paid a trip and those who continued on had to go up in the town.

Hamson approached him, saying in a low voice:

"Listen, Jasper. The boss will entrust you with an order of mine to be delivered to the Bank of Marsland. It is something important that you must keep faithfully and carry hidden so that no one knows that you are traveling with you. Here, to show more interest in it.

And handed him a five dollar coin.

Then, saying goodbye to the head of the office, he went to the bank to pick up the bag that he handed over to Jasper.

The stagecoach had to be detained for an hour in the town. They had to change the shot for another of soda, take care of the mail and deliver the bags from the one that left for the interior, and the mayoral needed to regain his strength by having lunch, which he had not been able to do on the way.

At half past five the order to leave was given. The three travelers who were waiting in the room of the Casa de Postas climbed into the vehicle, and the mayoral hid the heavy leather sack inside his seat, grasping the reins and cracking the whip.

The four spirited horses pulled off powerfully and, amid new clouds of dust, left the plaza to line up the path that wound between the railway line and the river.

Jasper planned to reach Seneca around eight at night. The road, due to accidents that cut the straight line, could be calculated at eleven miles, but it had four powerful mounts that covered them in two and a half hours.

The stagecoach was rolling rapidly through a dry and uncultivated terrain, which seemed more like sand than earth and in some parts, the potholes forced the vehicle to tumble so alarmingly that they made the travelers screams of terror when they considered that one of them could overturn.

Jasper, with the dead pipe between his teeth and the reins tightly held in his callused left hand, guided the fiery shot with great confidence and was ruminating between teeth:

" Five dollars! I have never seen that banker toad so rude that he does not say good morning if he does not charge interest for giving them. What will you send here in this sack that worries you so much? I would bet my position in the stagecoach that it is money in quantity. If I were not an honest man as I am, he deserved that instead of delivering him to Marsland I should continue the journey to Cross, total, fifty more miles of travel and get lost in the mountains of Black Hills, in Dakota.

"I don't know what the bag will contain, but I'm sure I have more to earn by driving errands the few years I have left to live. It would be a blow to that old miser who would have to pay it out of his pocket. Lucky for him that I am Jasper and that fifty-five years of honorable life are not thrown into the river for a handful of dollars, even if it is a lot.

Suddenly he pulled the reins to his chest to contain the momentum of the fiery horses. They had left three miles behind, and now he had to cross a rough and winding path, full of potholes and bumps, that cut through undergrowth, clearings, and some conglomerates of twisted and ancient trees.

He headed down the path, tumbling dizzy and began to twist through the twists and turns of the narrow path, until he reached a bend that at the exit, violently, descended downhill, for half a mile later he came out again to the plain.

He was rounding the corner when a detonation vibrated dryly over the sharp tinkling of the bells. Jasper put his hands to his chest, half-throwing a terrible oath and tried to grasp the rifle that he had leaning on the right side of the seat, but without the strength to do so he leaned forward and fell on the rumps of the rear shot that, scared , tried to continue the gallop attacked by panic.

But two new detonations, which were mixed with the hysterical screams of the travelers, vibrated again.

One of the horses, hit in the neck, whinnied anguishly, putting his hands up to half lift the vehicle, and his companion, hit in the front right oar, faltered while trying to advance and fell to the ground dragging the wounded man.

They both kicked and whinnied in a confused heap, while the two leading horses tried to follow the path without success. Not only the weight of the stagecoach but the dead weight of their two companions on the ground, immobilized them making their efforts sterile.

The stagecoach was stranded almost leaning on a small slope that formed the path; and suddenly, with an elastic leap, a figure fell from the top of one of the trees near the carriage and advanced towards the stage wielding two enormous revolvers.

The three frightened travelers fell back on their seats with eyes wide with terror and hands clasped in an anguished plea, while the robber advanced threatening with his weapons.

The afternoon died in a sweet bluish gloom and in its indecisive light, all that the frightened travelers could recognize about their attacker was that he was a rather massive man, dressed in a dark leather jacket, blue trousers tucked into high riding boots. Around his neck, he wore a red scarf knotted. On the face another that covered him from the nose down, and on the eyes, the fallen wings of an old hat that did not allow to recognize any particular detail of him.

Furthermore, his hands, which must have been powerful, appeared encased in old denim mitten gloves, which covered half his forearm.

The robber approached the half-lying vehicle and, opening the door, ordered in a hoarse voice:

"Get down! Do not fear for your lives.

The three women, trembling, got out of the carriage and the robber hastily opened their luggage, searching them without finding anything of value in them.

Grunting curses, he turned and climbed into the box. Livid Jasper, had been thrown by the horses six meters back, where he remained in a crouched position in a pool of blood, and the outlaw, ascended to the top where only the mail bags went.

He ripped open the securities box, took out some packets of letters that he kept in his ample pockets, and then began to rummage over the seat, until when he moved the lid of it, he lifted it.

He thrust his arm into the leather sack he raised, weighing it up, and when he found no more valuables, he descended back to the ground.

He addressed the women ordering:

"Come up!

They obeyed, and when they were inside, the outlaw crossed to a dent in the embankment and from it brought out a fine-looking black horse from whose saddle hung a large traveling sack.

He thrust the leather sack into it, mounted his horse, and impetuously threw himself down the sloping path until he filtered down a trail that led off the embankment, disappearing before the wide eyes of the travelers.

★ ★ ★

Across the wide plain between the river and the railroad track led to Nirvay, a horseman rode in the gold of the setting sun, standing tall in his saddle, his eyes fixed on the plain.

He was a young man of good stature, flexible in the hips, broad in the chest, and tanned in the face, who felt the effort of a long walk in his clothes, judging by the dust he had stored in them.

The traveler was about twenty-three years old, was quick in his eyes, sympathetic in features, tough in the flesh and, apparently, a man acclimated to spending hours and hours on the chair without showing fatigue.

He wore the typical cowboy outfit and on the saddle, a magnificent Winchester was swaying, while at the waist he wore an impressive colt of 45.

Impatient to get to town soon, he gently stroked the flanks of his horse, murmuring:

Come on, Nevada, hurry up a little bit. In an hour and a half at the latest, you will have the opportunity to take a well-deserved rest. Nirvay is not far anymore and there awaits you a good shed and some good feed to recover from this long journey.

The horse seemed to understand him because he quickened his trot, and shortly after, the rider managed to distinguish the features of the terrain that formed the path that led to the village.

Suddenly he stiffened. It had seemed to him, to catch the buzz of some detonations far away and looked everywhere uneasily, without discovering anything abnormal, but that sensation was sure that it had not been a delusion of his senses, but a tangible reality.

He was too used to picking up the roar of weapons to be confused and not specify when a revolver really thundered, or some similar noise could cause confusion, in that sense.

Restless, he murmured:

" Ray! Someone shot not far from here. I would swear it was in the clearing part. I'll have to make sure.

And he tightened the horse's trot even more, heading swiftly towards the pine path.

When he finally reached the average of this, he issued an oath and his eyes flashed with anger. He had just discovered the coach half leaning against the slope, the horses fallen in a pool of blood, while those who had escaped the attack unharmed kicked and neighed nervously with their legs trapped between the harness, and just beyond, bent over the hard earth , three frightened women, who moaned with tragic gestures next to a bundle that lay motionless on the ground.

The young man threw the horse almost on top of them, forcing them to run in terror, always screaming like chased rats and realizing that the bundle was a human body, he roared:

"Be still, a thousand rays, do not be scared that I am not an outlaw! What the heck has happened here?

The most complete of the three, the farmer's daughter, who had to get off a mile later, came forward stammering:

"Oh gallop, sir, he just disappeared over there, I might still catch up with him!

"Who?" Asked the traveler, puzzled.

"The robber. Not ten minutes ago he disappeared down that trail. Ride a black horse. He killed the mayoral, searched our luggage and the stagecoach and took a sack that he took from there ... from the seat ... Gallop for all the saints, and you can catch up with him!

The traveler without waiting for further supplications, roared:

"Wait! I will return in search of it.

And pressing his spurs on the horse's flanks, he urged him on:

Come on, Nevada, don't let it be said that you can't catch up with a four-legged black devil like you who's only ten minutes ahead of you.

The horse, as if it had been wounded in the most sensitive fiber of its pride, started like an exhalation and, in a few minutes, overcoming a hostile terrain not conducive to developing its brave speed, it crossed the embankments and went out to the plain facing the direction of the river. about four miles away.

"Nevada", in a straight line, as if it were contesting an important race, devoured a couple of miles at a fantastic gallop. Behind him, a cloud of dust was erasing his step, while the rider, with clenched teeth, his energetic chin a little protruding and his eyes fixed on the plain, angrily gripped the barrel of his rifle, wishing to discover a moving point on which to shoot.

As he approached the river, he could feel it in the damp, dirt-laden air that hit his face in the insane run, and he feared that if he did not catch up with the outlaw before he crossed the Missouri, it would be impossible to locate him, first, because of the darkness that was becoming more and more accentuated, and second, because the other shore covered with brush and trees, lent itself to conceal the persecuted.

Half a mile later, his keen eyes finally discovered the fugitive. It galloped almost as fast as he and with an effort of a mile and a half, it would reach the river and leave him outwitted.

The young man asked his horse for maximum effort and, grasping the rifle by the butt, he prepared to shoot the moment he had the outlaw within range.

The latter must have noticed the pursuit, because it seemed to increase the speed of his trot and, between them, a struggle was established that could only be decided by the lightest and most resistant horse of the two.

But the limit of the race was very short. The river was a magnificent aid to the fugitive and a terrible enemy to the pursuer. They both must have known, because they were both struggling to win the crazy short race.

But "Nevada" seemed lighter, because its rider roared with joy as he watched it gain distance. Before long, she would have him within range of her rifle and fire at him using her accurate aim.

And finally fired. The smoke from the shot hid the rider for a moment and when he discovered him again, he observed that he had missed. The mobility of both was great and the distance, as well as the gloom, too many.

But he received the reply. A bullet whizzed past him, warning that his enemy also knew how to handle a weapon.

This spurred the traveler's rage. He wasn't scared of angry people; on the contrary, it grew when it had to deal with great enemies.

The river was already in sight. The slightly cloudy ribbon of the Missouri shone like a wide sheet of steel in the fading light of the afternoon, and the young man fired again without success.

The fugitive's horse jumped into the water raising a whirlwind of black foam as it fell and swam eagerly towards the opposite shore, while the young man, prodding his mount, threw it towards the river, to cross behind him.

But in the momentum and when he was almost on the shore, "Nevada" stepped wrongly on a concealed hole and, bowing his hands, nailed his nose to the ground, throwing his rider by the ears. It rolled like a ball and got up furiously, trying to get back on its feet so as not to let its prey escape, when it was almost within reach.

But with deep despair, he observed that his mount had injured its leg as it fell. Blood was dripping from her and he did not dare to put her down on the ground, perhaps because the pain prevented him.

Furious, he abandoned his horse and ran to the riverbank. The outlaw had crossed it and his horse was pressing to go to the opposite bank.

He raised the revolver and fired. It was the last chance she had to stop him.

This time, the projectile was more accurate and was about to stop the escape of the outlaw forever; but because of a strange movement that the horse made to secure its front legs on the shore, when bending its hands, the projectile stuck in the saddle, under the back of the fugitive.

By a rare coincidence, when the bullet struck, it must have cut the strap of the travel bag that hung from the leather, because the young man observed perfectly how the bag drained and buried itself in the water, next to the shore, raising a wide whirlpool at the edge. sink. When he fired again, the horse had gained ground and was lost among the trees, taking refuge in them and in the raised bank that protected him.

The young traveler gave up the pursuit hopelessly. When his horse failed him, he had lost all possibility of it and when the pursuit was seriously wanted to be organized, God would know where the robber would already hide.

Worried, he returned to his horse. The animal was whinnying in pain and the young man anxiously examined its injured leg, but soon found that there was no bone fracture. He had suffered a painful scrape that forced him to bleed and perhaps a blow that caused him serious pain, but with a good rest and some arnica treatments, he would be new again.

And taking him by the bridle, not daring to mount it so as not to aggravate his situation, he returned to the scene of the tragedy, patiently walking the path that separated him from the stagecoach.

CHAPTER III

A LITTLE ENCOUNTER

When he reached the path again, the night had completely closed and the three frightened travelers, full of panic, not only because of the shock they had received but because they were alone in the dark next to the corpse of the mayoral, they longed for his return.

When they saw the young man appear with the horse by the bridle and bleeding, their fear increased and a stammering question:

"Are you… also… injured?

"No, fortunately not, but my horse is. He was unlucky enough to stumble when that bandit was within reach and this prevented me from reaching him. He crossed the Missouri and disappeared among the accidents on the other shore ... It was a pity!

Reacting, he added:

"Well. You cannot stay here. I cannot go to the village to ask for help, because my horse could not hold me in the saddle, so I am going to see how I can put the two horses that have been useful to use and I will guide the stagecoach to Nirvay. Is the only way.

One of the travelers hinted at an observation.

"You seem to know this side of the region.

"A little," replied the young man, smiling in the dark. It might come as a surprise to see me get there leading this hulk.

He pulled out a knife and cut the harness on the rear shot, freeing the two useful horses. Then he made the coach back up, hooked them up in the position of the two fallen, and left the carriage ready to roll. Everything ready, he forced the travelers to get into the carriage. He could not commit himself to go on to Seneca, seventeen miles distant, but he could go back and return them to Nirvay, until there they reorganized the service and looked for a new driver.

As for the corpse of the unhappy driver, he hoisted it over the top, at the cost of great efforts, to save the troubled women from having to travel in the company of the dead man and tying his horse to the back of the carriage, took the reins and resumed the village road at a moderate pace, so as not to cause damage to his own mount.

It was after nine o'clock at night when he saw the lights of the town and an intense emotion seized him when he saw them. He had long dreamed of his arrival on Nirvay, but he never dreamed that his entry into it would be so dramatic and spectacular.

The unexpected tinkling of the bells, heard from the plaza as they advanced along the dusty path, caused a deep sensation. No stagecoach was expected that night and from the head of the Casa de Postas to the last neighbor who passed through the square, they ran to the road, driven by curiosity.

Until someone, recognizing the carriage, shouted in dismay:

"It's Jasper's stagecoach coming back... and he's not driving it!

A crowded nucleus of onlookers pounced on the carriage when it stopped in front of the replacement station and Caster, the head of the service, came forward full of deep concern to inquire about the cause of this unusual return.

The light from the two lamps hanging over the office door reflected on the dark face of the young man who was guiding the vehicle, and Caster, widening his eyes, exclaimed:

"Frank Neil!

The latter, with an elegant leap, descended to the ground and, advancing towards him, exclaimed:

"Indeed, Mr. Caster, I am Frank. I see that, despite my long absence, I am still known in this town.

The chief, after the first moment of surprise, somewhat quenched the effusiveness he had put into the exclamation and coldly replied:

"Indeed, you are still known and people have not forgotten about you. What I do not understand is how you return on that stagecoach in which you had lost nothing.

"That's right, I hadn't lost anything in it, because I was coming on horseback, there you can see mine half lame behind, but when a man comes across a raided stage on a road, with two dead horses, the mayoral also dead and three unhappy panicked women, the least you have to do is help them. I've done it for them, Mr. Caster, and not for the Missouri Company.

Caster, who had changed color when he heard him, roared:

What are you saying, Frank? That the stage has been robbed and that Jasper ...?

"In there you have the travelers who can give you as many details as you want, and regarding Jasper, his corpse can be picked up from the top where I placed it.

Then, pointing up, he added:

"You will also find a torn bag. The robber appears to have made a thorough search.

Caster, turning pale, lunged for the box and with a trembling hand lifted the seat cover, revealing the empty interior. Dismayed, he descended, stammering:

"God of God! They have taken the leather bag!

"What does he get?" Asked Frank, intrigued.

"One that Mr. Hamson sent to Marsland. I don't quite know how much money it contained, but I reckon it was at least fifty thousand dollars!

The curious raised their hands to their heads in dismay. This was too serious a thing not to be moved. Very few were the criminal acts that had been carried out in the town, but this one was worth many blows that could be given in a long time.

Since another time, when there was also a mysterious robbery at the Bank, from which twenty thousand dollars in bills for the payment of the railway line workers disappeared, similar events had not happened again and the people, scared, detached themselves from the stagecoach forming circles where the event was discussed and that soon afterwards expanded through the town to spread the news to all corners of it.

Frank busied himself with helping the travelers to descend, accompanying them to the waiting room of the Post Office where he had to wait for Caster's resolution, and he, undone, livid, without being able to take any action, circled around the vehicle. , stroking his hair and talking to himself.

Frank stopped him in his tracks, yelling:

"What the hell are you doing standing there? Why don't you take care of those three poor women and the corpse of the mayoral? Are you stupid?

Caster tried to compose himself and muttered:

"Yes, yes... it's true... I must... but... by the hell!... Do you realize the seriousness of the case? Fifty thousand dollars from Banco Ganadero ...

"What the hell does it matter to me? What is that amount for the mean and selfish Mr. Hamson, who all his life has succeeded exploiting people? Let him pay them and burst! I wish they robbed him at the bank and even took his shirt on!

"Well, you talk like that because... well, this is not the time to argue. Help me if you want to lower the corpse. Then the sheriff will have to be accounted for. I hope you will be here to testify.

"I will or I will not be, but the sheriff will know where to find me. I have been absent from the village for more than three years and I have not come to save the interests of that Hamson's toad, or to take care of him, but to see my father. I think it is before anyone else and I did enough with chasing the outlaw I was about to hit, if my horse had not tripped and fallen, hurting his leg. If my horse becomes lame, Hamson will not come to make up for the loss.

"Well, let's not discuss that, Frank. You always so impetuous. Now it is a question of helping justice without looking in favor of whom it is done.

Caster began yelling for two grooms in the spare horse sheds, and between them and Frank lowered the corpse of the foreman.

Moved to the room amid the horror shown by the travelers, it was when, in the clear light of the lamps, Frank was able to appreciate how the driver had been injured. The bullet had gone through his neck, and the young man, examining the body, said:

"I don't understand much of this, but from the shape of the wound, I would swear it was hunted in passing, from a high place. The bandit must have been in ambush on the slopes or perhaps among the branches of a tree. That the doctor will tell you with more certainty.

Caster covered the body with a blanket and ordered one of the employees to go in search of the sheriff, which was no longer necessary, because when word spread about what had happened, someone had rushed to inform the first authority, and she was already going to the Casa de Postas to intervene in the event.

Frank, his mission accomplished, was about to leave the office to go home, when the sheriff's presence cut him off.

The current chief of police was not the same one the star wore when he left town, but he was also known to him. It was Edward Lang, who owned a saddler's workshop in the village.

Edward, when confronted with Frank, warned:

"Wait a minute, Frank, it looks like you are about to leave.

"That's right, Mr. Lang. I've been away from here for three years and I've only come to hug my father. I think I have a right to it.

"Indeed, Frank, and nobody disputes it with you, but I hope your good judgment will delay your visit a bit. Something serious has happened in which you have intervened in a spectacular way and I hope you do not want to refuse to give your help to justice.

"Of course not. I have already said that I was going to hug my father and then they had me at their disposal.

"Well, postpone the visit a bit. If that makes you happy, I'll tell you that your father is in perfect health and that his business is going from strength to strength. With this, I think you can resign yourself to waiting a few minutes.

Frank reluctantly obeyed and pulling out his pipe, he jammed it while the sheriff pestered him with questions.

Concise, he replied:

"Look, Lang, ask those ladies, they are the ones who can best inform you. I arrived when the robber was already fleeing towards the river.

The sheriff heeded the advice and questioned the travelers. They explained to him how the stagecoach had been robbed and all the maneuvers that the outlaw had carried out.

Since Caster had only words to regret the theft of Hamson's leather jacket, the sheriff asked:

"Who knew that this important bag was traveling in the stagecoach?

"I do not know. Of course me and the mayoral. Hamson brought it here in person when the stage arrived and reported it to me secretly in my office. I secretly communicated it to Jasper when I handed it over to him and I don't know more. Mr. Hamson will know if ...

"You have to notify him immediately" said the sheriff "is the most interested in the matter.

"It can't be," said the head of the Post Office. " He waited until the arrival of the coach full of anxiety, because he had to leave immediately. As he told me in a confidential way, he had an important meeting with a certain personality for something big that affects the region and ... I don't know more.

"Well, it would be very important to know who knew the exit of that bag ... that depends on following a clue.

Frank chimed in to say:

"I suspect you are astray, Sheriff. In the first place, I do not believe that Hamson gave two cents to the town crier announcing that he was sending that money through such an exposed channel, and second, that judging by what the travelers declare, the finding was accidental. The robber searched them, searched the bags of mail and lastly, requisitioning the stagecoach, found the hiding place. Had he known this detail and was the motive for the assault, he would have worried about looking for it in the first place. The rest should not be worth it.

The sheriff pondered the logic of such words and said:

"I think you're right, Frank, but… well, it's thinking of everything. Now tell us your story. You chased the outlaw.

"Indeed, it was. They told me that it had not been ten minutes since he had fled and I thought I had reached him.

Then he recounted his entire odyssey and how the fall from his horse had prevented him from hunting the fugitive.

What fell silent was his belief that the leather sack had been washed away. This was a detail that was reserved for investigation in due course.

His hatred for the man who had cut short his life and his illusions was so great that he preferred to let that money be lost and be paid for by the banker's private pocket, than to facilitate his rescue, if possible, although he did not trust that this would be the case. was.

When he finished his story, the sheriff asked:

"Do you have any ideas that will help you at some point recognize the robber?

"None. I intervened in the late afternoon, when the sun had already sunk below the horizon and twilight reigned. I was able to appreciate, like the travelers, that he was a broad-shouldered man, of regular stature, rather tall and wearing high boots. He was riding an all black horse and I can't be more precise.

"Well. I will provide details to the neighboring towns for my colleagues to investigate. Perhaps someone has seen him cross in some direction. It is not an easy thing if you are far ahead and cross the divide. Dakota and Wyoming are very close and there ...

Frank impatiently interrupted:

"Well, Mr. Lang," he said, "I think I have told you how much I could contribute to your work. If you like, before I go, you can examine my horse and see that its leg has been injured in pursuit. You can also see my rifle, which is missing a shell, and my revolver, which has three bullets.

"Wait a minute," interrupted the sheriff. What caliber are your weapons?

"The Winchester is a 40.70 centerfire and the revolver a .45 Colt. Does it have something to do with the death of that unfortunate man?

The sheriff blushed a little. Frank's question had been impetuous and threatening.

"No ... I don't think ... but it is good to have as many details as possible.

Frank ironically added:

"If that's why, you can also measure my footwear and my horse's hooves. Then, he puts everything in a hat, shakes it, takes something out of it and ... solved the case.

Lang looked at him sternly, replying:

"Frank, I see you come back as impulsive and mocking as you left. You have forgotten many things ...

"You are wrong, Lang, I have not forgotten any. Perhaps it is something that people regret.

"As long as it doesn't weigh you down too ...

"Well, if that's the case, too bad. Do you need anything else from me?

"Not. You can leave, but I hope you won't be leaving so soon that I don't have a chance to see you again.

"I'm afraid I won't go, Lang. Maybe this is the bad thing.

And he went towards the exit, at the moment when the door was opened violently and the tall and blond silhouette of a young woman, pretty and elegant, was outlined in the frame.

Frank, as if he had been bitten by an asp, stepped back, feeling a rush of blood rush to his dark face, while the newcomer, seeing him, turned pale, exclaiming:

"Frank!

He made a mighty effort to compose himself and replied:

"Indeed, Sylvia. I am Frank Neil. I thought that after three years of absence you would no longer remember me.

"It is one thing to remember and another to remember. They had told me that … but, sorry. There is something urgent that I need to clarify.

And turning to the head of the Post Office, he asked vehemently:

"What is running through town, Mr. Caster? They have told me that the stage has been robbed and that the mayoral has been killed.

"That's right, Miss Hamson," replied the boss, confused, pointing to Jasper's body hidden by the blanket. " There you have it.

She backed away, making a look of horror in her pretty mouth and then added:

"Awful, Mr. Jasper, awful! But … I have been told more … Is it true that my father had sent a leather sack with fifty thousand dollars on the stage and that it has disappeared?

"It is true, Miss Hamson. The sack has disappeared, but as for the amount it contained, I do not know. Didn't you know?

"No," she replied confused. " My father did not speak to anyone about the shipment … not even to me. He only told me that he had to be absent until Monday for a very important conference and I don't know where. My God, fifty thousand dollars! How upset he is going to be when he finds out!

"Indeed, it is not a trivial handful of dollars.

"And… the robber could not be located?

The sheriff pointing at Frank, warned:

"Yes, Miss. Frank arrived at the scene shortly after and galloped in pursuit of the robber. It caught up with him near the river, but … his horse stumbled and fell as the fugitive crossed the stream. He fired at him several times, but missed him.

"Yes, it is strange," said Sylvia sarcastically, "that Frank Neil, a man who has always bragged about being a gunman, missed shots at a distance that would not exceed thirty yards! There are amazing things!

Frank felt all his blood catch fire at her comment. She had done nothing to deserve the scorn of someone who had always been a good friend, and now, hearing him accuse in that scathing way in front of people, a dull rage flooded her soul.

Enraged, he turned, exclaiming:

"You have become an aggressive, silly, moron lady, Sylvia! I see that you are a worthy daughter of your father and that he has instilled in you his stupid theories and his foolish pride of an ambitious man, without merit to be so. Rancher raised by money, he forgets his origin and wants to erase yours from your blood, as if that were possible. I have never bragged about being a gunman and you know it.

«I have boasted of only a man and of a whole man and without dreams of greatness that do not suit me. If you said that with a clutter, it is not worth taking into consideration. If you had been a man ...

An altered voice called out from the door ...

"She is not a man, Frank, and that is why you presume to be, but here is a man willing to answer for her.

Frank angrily turned his eyes to the door. In it, and covering almost the entire span, the silhouette of Dennis Powell, Sylvia's boyfriend, stood out.

Dressed in cheesy and affected elegance, he looked more than a wealthy local rancher, an exotic stranger from the East trying to roughly adapt to the customs and garb of the region. It was like an unrepentant figurine trying to modify clothes with aristocratic airs in bad taste.

Frank angrily took two steps forward saying:

"You a man? You have not been your whole life more than a silly child, spoiled to walk your ridiculous figure around the town and dazzle young foolish women like this one. The men here will be ashamed to know that you intend to represent them.

Dennis, red as sagebrush, jumped on Frank trying to apply his robust fists to his face, while Sylvia, scared, screamed to stop him, but the farmer's son's attempt did not go beyond there ...

Frank flexed his waist slightly, avoided the blind blow, and extended his right arm like a powerful spring, applied it to the mouth of his assailant, sending him backward against the door.

Dennis collided with the frame, gave a roar of pain and collapsed like a wimp, while Sylvia, terrified, covered her face with her hands, believing that her boyfriend had been undone from the terrible impact.

Lang tried to grab Frank, but Frank, sharply pushing him away, roared:

"Leave me, Lang, leave me; you have witnessed me being insulted and Frank Neil is not insulted by anyone.

CHAPTER IV

HAMSON STARTS HIS ATTACK

The announcement of Frank Neil's arrival was as if a bomb had dropped in the village. Three years was not long to erase from people's memories memories that, though dormant, remained perennial, and soon the details of his life were resurrected again until the moment when he disappeared from Nirvay.

The rumor spread as a result of his departure about his performance in the theft of cattle, revived again in the memory of some and although the tests had not been very satisfactory, popular slander always admits the bad more easily than the good and everyone is they stood guard against him, waiting for the sheriff's attitude to take on this old affair.

On the other hand, it was very coincidental that he was a leading figure in the Missouri stagecoach robbery issue. Nirvay was a meek and quiet town, where armed robberies and violent deaths turned out to be exotic flowers, and that bloody event "the bloodiest that was remembered in the place" had to unfold precisely when Frank was returning to the town.

Soon the story of her performance was increased and corrected by word of mouth, and many "as Sylvia had done", welcomed her statements with reservations. An individual like him, an excellent marksman, could not take three shots at such close range and the fact that this could have happened gave rise to certain doubts.

Throughout the day of the following Sunday, the comments were for all tastes. The young people, as well as the old, forgot their favorite amusements "some dancing and others taverns" and in groups in the square, on the main street, or in the establishments, they dedicated themselves to forming hypotheses about the event and drawing from he particular conclusions, few of which favored the newly returned nomad.

He did not appear in the town all day Sunday. Tired of the long day and bitter about the scenes that had followed his return, he spent the day sleeping, and when he got up, he did not want to leave the home of his father, at whose side he spent the evening recounting his hazardous exploits in the West.

Regarding the matter of the assault on the stagecoach, he told him everything that had happened, except the incident of the sack. It seemed as if something was forcing him to keep quiet about the matter, although he did not attach great importance to it either, as he was sure that the sack had been lost in the muddy waters of the Missouri.

On Monday morning, Hamson returned to his pretty suburban farm. He seemed tired from the trip, but satisfied with the result.

He found his daughter nervous and with signs of having cried and when he tried to inquire about the motives of those accusing traces, she, feverish, gave him an account of everything that had happened.

The banker screamed at the news of the loss of money and the incorrect and brutal manifested by Frank. He could not forgive her returning and treating her daughter so contemptuously, although deep down he was glad that the unexpected encounter had developed in such a cold and aggressive way.

This had just erased all traces of the past between them and left the future clearly clear. Sylvia and Frank could no longer even be two discreet friends.

As for the incident with Dennis, he was furious. After all, under the false cloak of "makeshift knight," the blood of the West throbbed in him and the air of turbulent rancher life, and it sickened him that his future son-in-law had suffered such a defeat and humiliation.

Furious, he roared:

"What kind of mud is Dennis made of that didn't destroy Frank? He insulted you in front of the sheriff and if he had destroyed him right there, Lang would have had to agree with him.

"But, Dad" she replied confused "Dennis wanted to come out in my defense and his own. He was unarmed and jumped on Frank to cover his mouth with his fists.

"And he let his cover up, didn't he? Such a situation cannot remain like this! I admit that Dennis is not a thug, nor a gunman like Frank, but he is a man and he must prove it. I cannot allow my daughter's future husband to go through the humiliation of having been beaten without taking revenge. You must understand it and so does he.

"Okay, Dad, okay, but Dennis hasn't had time to get himself together ... when he's restored ... we'll see ... You know who Frank is ...

"I know who Frank is and he will know who I am ... He has come back only to make my life bitter, he does not forgive me for rightly opposing your intimate friendship. He believed that I was just a rough rancher who had not known his intention and I did. I was trying to abuse your innocence to trick you, marry you and take over my capital living at the expense of both of us ... No ...! I could not consent to it and I am glad that you reacted by realizing who it is. On the other hand, there is much to discuss on the matter of the theft of my money ...

«I admit that he, absent, did not know that I was going to carry out the shipment, but ... who tells me that I did not agree with the robber to give the blow to the stagecoach? He knows this, he knows that the mail usually carries Securities, perhaps they agreed to steal it and chance made them trip over the bag ... Fifty thousand dollars ...! That is the amount Sylvia, and if she shares it with that outlaw, she will be able to boast of having made money out there and settle here and try to make my life bitter ...

No ... He won't. I have a lot of inquiries to do. His assertion that he chased the robber and shot him without hurting him, losing sight of him, is childish ... As if we don't know how that guy knows how to handle a revolver!

"What do you mean by that, Dad? Sylvia asked, intrigued.

"Much and nothing, but, one of two; Either it is a lie that he chased the outlaw or he faked it to justify his intervention in the matter ... I'll have to make him tighten the pegs until he sings the truth.

"That's very strong dad, you can't accuse him without evidence.

"No evidence? Is it not raining on wet? Who stole those cattle from me as soon as I disappeared from the town?

"It couldn't be proven, Dad... Scott said he was almost certain he recognized Frank, but because of the darkness he might have been confused.

"He wasn't confused... He was afraid that Frank might retaliate on him. He is a bully and bullies are often saved from the gallows because of the fear of others, but I am not afraid of him or of anyone. I do not forget that I have been a rancher and I have seen them face to face many times with the cattle rustlers.

"Well, Dad... Don't get excited. Now the main thing is to be able to locate the robber. The authorities must do something.

" Something...! I would if I had authority. I would force Frank to speak ... He has to know ...

"Dad!" Sylvia exclaimed annoyed without knowing why. I think you're going too far. I allowed myself to doubt the truth that he said to expose and I saw how he reacted furiously ... Why couldn't it have happened as he says?

"Are you going to defend him now? The banker roared, fearing that his daughter still had an embers of sympathy for Frank.

"No, but I don't want you to go to extremes that I can confront him with him. Such an accusation could exasperate him and ... it scares me to think of the consequences.

"Do not worry. You'll see how the lion is not as fierce as people paint him. I know how to handle the matter.

"Well, what about the money?

"That's the worst, Sylvia. I have a feeling that something unpleasant is going to happen to the local ranchers and settlers. That money was theirs, I, in my capacity as Director, have to order the distribution of funds and use the only existing means to transfer the money. If there is no security, what is my fault? Am I going to lose it? No ... And this is what I have to get into their heads.

"Bad business, dad. They will say that their money has been kept in the Bank for their safety and that the one you moved outside was not theirs.

"Well, whose is it, perhaps mine? All the money I keep belongs to everyone and it affects everyone. We'll see what happens, but don't count on me putting it out of my pocket. Find it and return it. I'll call a shareholders' meeting and we'll see how it ends.

And furious, he marched to the bank where he remained, all morning, locked up without wanting to see anyone.

The event, although it had caused the indignation of the people, had not sowed the alarm, because no one thought that it could reflect in their current accounts. They all believed in good faith that this was a matter for the Director, who was obliged to watch over the deposits and who should be responsible for their integrity.

When the bank closed, Hamson was forced to go to the sheriff's office. He had sent word to visit him and Hamson came in a fury.

"This is a real scandal, Lang!" Was his first comment. " You are the sheriff of the village and you remain so calm in your offices without knowing that the robbers haunt Nirvay like ants in the trees. Do you realize your responsibility?

"Why?" Replied the sheriff annoyed. Were there any signs of outlaws in the vicinity?

"Is there a place in the West where they don't exist? I find you very clueless, Lang.

"It will be your opinion. On the other hand, did you tell me that you were planning to make such a dangerous shipment?

"Did I have to advertise my transactions?" Roared the banker. " If taking it in the greatest secret that has happened, what would have happened to walking around with the jacket showing it to everyone?

"Don't screw things up, Mr. Hamson. It was enough that he had warned me. I personally would have accompanied the stage to Seneca.

" And that? Perhaps you owe me my life for not warning you, but at best, assuming you were taken for an ogre, the blow would have come later. No, Lang, the money was destined to disappear, because thieves hadn't disappeared before!

"It was a fortuitous event. I believe that not even the robber himself dreamed of the importance of the blow he was going to deliver.

" Not? And what about Frank's intervention? He left when cattle was stolen from my pasture and was recognized by one of my peons; He comes back when fifty thousand dollars is stolen from me and intervenes in the strangest way ... I hope you have not believed any of that absurd story he has told.

"How can I support myself for this?

"Simply in his background. His performance is very dark and I happen to believe that he was in combination with the robber.

"To steal his leather jacket?

"Not precisely for that, but to rob the stage and steal the values of the mail. I suspect that he came with a colleague and as he is known here, he sent him to strike, waiting to help him. When he saw him triumph, he presented himself as a savior of travelers and to justify his arrival.

He knew they would tell him that the robber had just fled and pretended to pursue him. Surely she accompanied him to the river to facilitate his escape and guide him. I'd keep a close eye on Frank. I am convinced that one day or another he will seek out his partner to claim his share of the loot. Then he will say that he has made money in the West and that he is coming to settle ... What do you know of his wanderings out there?

" Nothing! Why did I have to take care of him?

"Sure, but ... you'll see how it is. My heart tells me.

"Well, I haven't let his hand go yet. I will harass him with questions, I will force him to realize his life, and above all, of his steps when he returns and I will have him watched ... I cannot do more, because without a test it is not lawful to detain him.

"Well, he may regret not doing it. One day it will slip from his hands like eels and he will go with my money to succeed there and live splendidly.

"We will make sure that it is not so. I've placed orders across the region to investigate. Someone must have seen a rider on a black horse.

" A lot of! And they will arrest a hundred citizens who ride horses of that color ... You yourself could be arrested if you left for having a black horse. I have two, Isaac White has one ...

"Okay, but there are no more indications. That is, the leather jacket remains.

"That they are not going to wear it around their neck to display as a trophy. The bag will one day appear empty in a ravine and there history will have died.

The sheriff, beset by Hamson's pessimism, asked:

"Can you think of any other steps to discover the author?

"If I were a sheriff, I would think of many, because I would not be afraid to act. First of all, I'd put Frank in jail.

"I can not do it.

"Not even for the theft of my cattle?

Not for that. It did not happen during my tenure and as far as I know, it was not reliably proven.

" Already! As this will not be proven. The waiter is clever, but Lang, step on your feet. If you do not resolve soon and well, I will have to use my influence in the contour so that a more capable and energetic sheriff is appointed. Rumine this, that interests you.

"Well, you can do it, I don't dispute it. If you want a sheriff to suit you, let them appoint him, but I am made to measure of justice nothing more and nothing less.

Hamson, shocked, got up, shouting:

"Is it a challenge, Lang?

"It is a reason. I will do what I deem necessary, but I will not go so far as to throw dirt in my eyes for anyone.

"Well. He will remember that threat.

And furious, he left the offices, leaving the sheriff even more furious than he was.

The banker's irascibility was heightened during the afternoon hours that he continued to work at the Bank, and thus, when night fell, he returned to his farm, he was a shot who was about to explode in full swing.

The last person to suffer from Hamson's bile abscesses that day was Dennis, who, quite recovered from the blow suffered the night before, had come to visit Sylvia and to testify to the banker for the loss suffered.

When Hamson fixed his fierce eyes on the dapper young man's face and discovered the marks of the terrible blow on his swollen lips, he looked at him sternly, saying:

"What the heck kind of man are you, Dennis? Is he one of those who, following Christian maxims, when he receives a slap, puts the other cheek to receive the second? If so, I doubt that you have another mouth to offer it and that they put it on as they have given you the only one they have.

Dennis, red with shame, exclaimed:

"Mr. Hamson, you are unfair. I came out in defense of his daughter and wanted to punish that guy, but I missed the blow and didn't have time to answer his. I don't think I have shown fear.

"But yes, nullity, which for the case is the same. I don't like that, Dennis. Whoever aspires to get my daughter's hand must be a man in every sense of the word. I admit I caught you off guard and crushed your face, but what have you done since last night?

"Nothing, but I will. I am in pain and have to think about how I resolve the matter. You know that I am not a gunman; I wield a gun like many, but not like Frank. If I were so stupid that I looked for a revolver at his belt, it would be as much as committing suicide by someone else's hand.

"Well, what is my fault that his father did not know how to educate him for the West? Is this a butterfly nest? Here you have to defend yourself with ingenuity and weapons. I am an educated man for society because I decided to do so and that is why I have reached the brilliant position that I have; But I also learned to handle defensive weapons as God commands, so that no one abuses me because they see me wearing a frock coat, a fancy vest and a white collar shirt with a scarf.

'You just took care of the dress and you're not going anywhere with that, Dennis. I'm sorry to tell you, because I appreciate you very much and I have given you belligerence to woo my daughter, but from that to happen because one day I won't be able to defend her if someone insults her, not that. You have been humiliated in the eyes of all, you cannot forget that and only by washing the offense will you regain the esteem of the people.

«Ingest them for it and do not forget that since you are the one offended, you have the right to take the initiative. That is a great advantage to avoid a lot of fuss with the sheriff. If you have something on your mind, you will understand what I am saying and act accordingly.

And without wanting to hear more reasons, he left everything confused and ashamed to lock himself in his office.

Dennis came to Sylvia for a palliative and help, but her mood was no better than her father's. She had listened to his entire diatribe and although she had refined her education in a school, she was still a woman of the region, in which the blood of the West and its atavisms could not be denied.

To the young man's lamentations, he replied:

"I'm sorry, Dennis, but I can't take my father's reason. I admit that Frank caught you off guard and knocked you down with one blow, but you can't just leave it like this ... Don't you understand that you would be the mockery of the town?

"It's okay, Sylvia. I did not say that I try to avoid an encounter with that wild cowboy, but ... I have to watch how I do it. Frank is a gunman and I'm not up to him with a gun in hand.

"But you have two fists, Dennis. I know Frank and I know that he is not capable of using weapons that his opposite is not capable of using. I do not know what he may have done, or what he can be accused of specifically, but I treated him for a long time and I could see that he always acted with nobility.

"Maybe he's 'the generous bandit.' A Jesse James or a Billy "the Kid" "commented wryly, Dennis.

"I don't know what it will be, nor do I care. That is over, but I am fair enough to abide by the truth.

"Okay, it looks like you guys have conspired to get me into a dangerous business. I am not a coward, I will show you more than anything, but although I am not a coward, I am not a madman who sticks his head in a stocks to be imprisoned.

And furious at the violence of that situation, he took his hat and left without saying goodbye.

CHAPTER V

WHAT A MAN CANNOT ENDURE

Frank spent the whole day of Sunday in the privacy of the home, with his father, who was giving him very valuable information on the life of the village during the three years that the young man had been absent.

They were data that, in addition to taking him back to a happier and more longing time than the present, would serve him well, since his purpose when he returned to Nirvay was to settle there permanently.

Old Neil, still strong and erect, satisfied all of his son's questions, especially regarding Hamson and his activities. The brand-new banker had been the cause of all his misfortunes, and Frank was coming back with the deliberate intention of repaying his past bad times, if possible, in spades. As for Sylvia, he had been deeply disappointed to find her so changed and so attached to her father's theories, plagued by delusions of grandeur.

A deep bitterness seized him at having been able to verify that the good friendship that united them, that outbreak of simple and healthy love that did not explode between them in words, but that had been tacitly admitted by one and the other, had not only dried up. and dead, but the poisonous root had turned into a contempt he could not admit.

Sylvia seemed no better or worse than her father. She had been seduced by the spectacle of greatness and was willing to sacrifice her heart and her youth to a stupid and foolish love, the magnitude of which had been measured by the capital that Dennis's father could possess.

Frank couldn't explain the change in her feelings. She knew Dennis as she had to know him, and without envy or passion, coldly studying the young man's conditions, she found in him nothing more than an empty and pampered guy, useful for showing off and spending, lacking any initiative and all nerves and so paid of his type and his sure heritage, that he had to sacrifice everything to the pose and the flash.

This was not a man of the West, nor could he ever be. All the fiber of the environment that he had breathed was dead in him, and if Hamson, who despite all his faults, was aggressive, tenacious and dynamic, he trusted that that conceited doll could one day take over the direction of his business, emerging with flying colors. the company, he was more than wrong.

Of course that was not his thing. Sylvia could choose whoever she wanted and do whatever she wanted with her heart, but she couldn't admit that she treated him with the aggression that she had treated him, nor looked so over her shoulder, when nothing had happened between them to justify such attitude.

Frank knew it was all Hamson's patient work, but it hurt him that she was made of such a malleable wax that he had been so impressed.

Well, now, all friendship with the young woman was broken, no obstacle prevented her from returning to the banker the blows that he had tried to give her. This was an unpaid debt, which he did not want to forget. Hamson had misjudged him as an enemy, judged him a sad ranch laborer with no other aspirations than to enjoy the capital of the banker through a marriage with his daughter, and he was going to prove him wrong. He was a true man of the West, with the nerves to carry out his aspirations and the time to make the show had come.

The three years he had spent outside of his hometown had been a hard but reproductive apprenticeship in life's teachings for him. Faced with good and evil, he had walked along the path that delimited them, looking for a way to make a fortune without it being favorable for a long time.

He had been a laborer on some ranches, a cattle shredder, a trusted man of a cattle dealer, with whom he managed to earn a few hundred dollars "the first savings of his life", and later, tired of the slowness in gathering an amount deserving of that waste of energy, she decided to gamble everything on one card.

The silver mines in Nevada seduced him. He did not understand mines, but he had muscle, tenacity, audacity and nerve, and using all his savings to acquire decent equipment, he took to the mountains in search of seams.

He had a moment of despair when his possibilities were exhausted before he discovered a tiny particle of the precious metal; until one day he came across a weak vein in a place where, a little later, silver began to flow lavishly.

The news of the discovery attracted an operating company and it began to acquire the concessions. There was a poor offer for poor Frank's lode, but Frank firmly rejected it. He was starving, he was about to be forced to give up the exploitation, but he did not want to give way to the company. He had guessed that this one needed his concession nestled in the heart of those already acquired, and he wanted to make it pay well.

There was a great struggle, until, locked in a number, he managed to be recognized when he no longer had the courage to resist. Fifty thousand dollars was his position and he wanted all or nothing.

When he received the check for the concession, he estimated that his wanderings in the West had ended, and one day, without warning, without any hurry, wishing to rest from so much fatigue on a gentle and pleasant journey through the region that saw him born. He returned to Nirvay on the back of his trusty horse, which he had not wanted to get rid of even in times of greatest hardship.

The check was deposited with the Bank of Marsland, the end of the Missouri stagecoach route. He had not yet decided what he would do with the capital and did not want to expose it to the public until the time was right. His idea was to acquire a ranch in the town and begin his aggressive campaign against Hamson. He had to study the vulnerabilities of the deified banker and when he had him, he would begin his offensive.

Neil's father, knowing his son, was afraid of his outbursts and advised him to restrain his nerves. Hamson was a very influential man in the village and he could cause her a new upset, as he tried to do when he had enough skill to accuse him of having tried to steal her cattle.

But Frank, laughing, answered his father:

"Do not worry about that. The West has taught me many things. I know how to fight on all terrains. If here I can't find someone who has the guts to confront me with a revolver in hand, I will holster it and make use of other kinds of weapons, but that does not mean that they will be less terrible. Sometimes it is better to die with dignity with a revolver in hand than to be exposed to die like a mangy coyote, stuck in a hole, despised by the people.

"What's your idea, Frank?" Asked the old man.

"I don't know yet, father; I have to orient myself. I prefer to have them in the belief that I return penniless. If they knew that I have money and that I intend to buy a ranch here, Hamson would use his influence to prevent it from being sold to me. I will wait. Ah! How are you doing money?

"If you need something to complete the purchase, you can have up to ten thousand dollars. The rest is invested in the warehouse.

"No, I won't need it. Where do you have the money?

"At Hamson's Bank; he had no other choice. Having taken him to Seneca, apart from how annoying it is to have to go there to carry out the transactions. Hamson would have boycotted my business.

"Well. This makes me happy in part, because it gives me the right to intervene in the banking operations of that toad. He trades with our money and that forces him to account.

Frank's father stiffened, suddenly asking:

"And now that you talk about trading. What is going to happen with that robbery?

" What do you mean?

"Simply, who is going to lose what was stolen.

" Ray! Who is going to lose it? Hamson ...

" You think? So, you don't know him anymore. During your absence, there was a robbery that still could not be cleared up. Someone was able to force a window, enter at night, and appropriate a few thousand dollars that the cashier had in his desk drawer for a payment that he had to make very early.

«Hamson summoned the account holders and made them see that the Bank did not have its own money, but that which was entrusted to it and that since the disappearance had been fortuitous and no one could be blamed, no one had to pay out of their private pocket the disappeared. The formula was to lower the small percentage of interest to the principal for a certain time, until it covered what was stolen.

"Hell's Bells!" Yelled Frank. That cannot be ... Who said that the Bank does not have its own money? Doesn't Hamson trade the deposits and use money in profitable business transactions? No ... He won't pretend that, but if he does, Nirvay is going to burn with all that it contains. It seems to me that this is going to be the weak point where the first live will be received. I'm glad you warned me of that.

The next day, Frank received a message from the sheriff to report to their offices. The young man, a little suspicious, responded to the call.

"Here I am, Mr. Lang," he said. Tell me what it is about.

The sheriff, after pondering the answer, asked:

"Let's see Frank, keep in mind that I do not prejudge anyone's performance and therefore, I do not prejudge yours, but do not forget that my mission is to investigate everything that happened to the last limit and draw consequences if possible and follow a clue if there is room for it.

"Very well, I do not dispute it.

"Therefore, I beg you not to exalt yourself and answer my questions with all sincerity. I am in a difficult situation and I confess that it is because of you. At the very least, help me solve it.

"For my sake? I do not understand you...

"Well, I'll speak to you clearly. Hamson is furious. I understand it because the case is to be. Do not forget that he bears a grudge against you for things that do not matter to me and that this and your untimely arrival in the village have aroused in him certain suspicions that he has tried to make me share, just because he conceived them.

"Because I have resisted, he has threatened to influence me to replace me, which I do not care, but I do care that there may not come a time when he can accuse me of not having fulfilled my duty to the limit.

"I want to understand you. What is it about?

"Where were you coming from when you got here?

"From Marsland.

"Can you justify it?

"If necessary, in a reliable way.

"Why did you come on horseback and not on the stage? The road is very long and tiring.

"True, but I had a horse that I neither wanted to sell nor abandon. On the other hand, until I got to Marsland, I have worked like an elephant, I have suffered hardships and hunger, I have had everything in my life and when the time has come for me to rest, I wanted to make the trip comfortable, calm and peaceful. I longed to come to hug my father and was afraid to come for many things of an intimate nature.

"Perhaps because of that accusation of the theft of cattle?

"That has never worried me. I knew it, because my father wrote it to me and if he had not picked up his letter very far from here and with a long delay, I would have returned to put a yearling with horns and everything in his mouth whom he would have had the cynicism to falsely accuse me. The matter is more intimate.

"I guess. I suppose you have realized that the matter died.

"Yes, but Hamson's work has not died.

"Let's put that down, Frank. Hamson and many people have found the coincidence of your arriving at the scene of the assault precisely ten minutes after the assault to be too strange.

" And because? The same thing could happen ten minutes before or have arrived at the right time. I will tell you that when I was about ten minutes away, the air brought the echo of several detonations in my ear, and attracted by them, I galloped to the path. When I arrived, the robber had leaked through a crevice in the slopes heading for the Missouri, and at the request of the frightened travelers who thought I could reach him, I tried to follow him. They can confirm that.

"They have certainly confirmed it, but there are those who suspect that the robber acted in agreement with you. That you gave him directions to rob the stage, to know the route and customs and that you showed up shortly after to justify the alibi. There are also those who do not believe that you, an excellent shooter, could miss your shots at such close range and that what you did was follow the robber, help him escape and make sure that the loot was good and that one day you would receive your share.

"Is it Hamson who suspects that? Frank asked, gnashing his teeth furiously.

"Think about it, why am I going to deny it?

" And you?

"I haven't gone that far yet, Frank. Before fixing that suspicion as possible, I have recalled your history and that of your father. You were always an impulsive and gruff boy, but honest. Your father too. It is true that when you left, the incident of the cattle theft occurred, but ... it went to Hamson and Hamson hated you. Why couldn't I find some false witness to discredit you?

«I have taken all of this into account before judging and, therefore, I have not wanted to heed Hamson's suggestions. He is sure that things turned out the way he thinks and that one day your part in the business will come to light.

Frank was tense. He was thinking that the day he made it known that he had money, precisely an amount equal to what had been stolen, those suspicions could be accentuated against him.

Annoyed by the thought, he warned:

"Does this mean that if I showed thousands of dollars now, would people believe they belonged to Hamson's stolen bag?

"Exactly, but since I suspect that you come so bald how you left ...

"Well, don't suspect it, Lang. I have money and precisely an amount equal to what was stolen, but fortunately, I can prove two things. First, where it came from and second, where it was deposited long before the assault occurred.

"Do you want to try it on?

"Yes sir, but on condition that you do not realize that I have that money and keep it for you ... I do not intend to display it until I need it.

"But then...

"Then, whoever wants to, accuse me. I can continue to show that it has nothing to do with the robbery, See.

From his portfolio, he extracted the contract for the assignment of his silver vein for the fifty thousand dollars and the document that had been delivered to him at the Bank of Marsland, when he made the deposit of the money.

"Does this satisfy you?

"If you don't have more money, yes.

"Not. I have no more, I swear.

"Well. Let this be forgotten. Now, remember. Could you not provide me with some information to carry out some procedure to help me resolve the matter? You'll be the first to win, Frank. You already know Hamson. He is capable of developing his theory for the whole town and his word will always be more believed than yours.

«It would be a violent situation for you if people, in doubt, admit you with reservations and believe in their hearts that you were an accomplice of the robber.

" Lightning and thunder! If he does that to me, I'll kill him.

"Take it easy. It is more positive to prove your mistake or slander. By killing him without providing any proof of your innocence, you would not anticipate anything.

"What proof can I provide if I don't have more?

"I do not know. That is why I tell you to make your memory work.

Frank was brooding. He understood the reasons of the sheriff, who was now behaving honestly and loyally with him, and tortured his brain to help him not only in his management, but for his own benefit.

Suddenly, he jumped on the seat and stood up, exclaimed:

"Listen, I'm going to try that test, but not now. Maybe it was not just for me, but for Hamson, and I don't want to benefit him at all. Before, I want to know his game and only when I am convinced of it, will I or will I be able to contribute it. It is something very improbable and for the same reason that I can fail, I do not tell you. Let him believe what he wants and use his tongue as he sees fit. One day I will make him bite it and poison himself with it.

"You are wrong not to tell me, Frank. I am showing you to treat you like a friend.

"And I appreciate it as you have no idea, but I do not want to risk failure and let you doubt that it was the epilogue of a story that is already taking too many flights. If I can provide that proof, you will be the first to know it, I promise you.

"Well, I will have to resign myself. The bad thing is that this way we cannot advance anything and Hamson will add fuel to the fire and things will get very tight. I am afraid that one day I will have to be angry with him, which will be as much as being angry with the position, and if I let him ... he thinks that he will appoint someone of his make to support his plans and give you a lot to do.

"I hope not. Stand firm and tell him that you are working on the case. I hope it won't take many days for him to give him that test or ... to fail and then ...

And with a mocking gesture, he left the offices.

CHAPTER VI

THE FIGHT

After leaving the sheriff's offices, he decided to walk around town, show up, cultivate old friends, and tap into public opinion. In three years of absence, things could have happened that he did not know and wanted to be aware of the climate of the inhabitants, to know exactly the possibilities he could count on when he began his offensive against Hamson.

He went directly to Oliver Kukon's bar, the most decent public establishment in the town, where merchants and industrialists used to meet to play dice or poker and exchange views on the market situation, or gossip a bit about the little ones. local incidents.

It was twilight, the lights of the establishment were beginning to shine against the blue gloom that hung over the dusty road, and the clientele, although not very numerous, was abundant.

As soon as he stepped through the door, he discovered several well-known faces. Pat, the barber, who when he didn't have a customer on his hands would hasten across the opening to soak his throat or gamble on the glass next to the dice; the blacksmith, who had already closed his establishment; Mr. Wilker, the pharmacist, unmistakable for his long, pointed nose and glasses that, rebelliously, struggled to play on the slide; Jackson, the owner of the haberdashery next to the bar, and several other customers who, now, when he confronted them again, made him forget that he had been absent for three years.

He also discovered two former peons from Hamson's ranch with whom he had lived amicably and others whose dealings he frequented less, but who were no strangers to him.

Frank expected a warm welcome from everyone. It was not that he thought they were going to cry with emotion when they saw him among them again, but he did believe that his old friendship gave him the right to expect a strong handshake from each one and a while of pleasant chat, taking an interest in their adventures.

His surprise was great and painful, when after his effusive greeting there was a dry and soft general reply and some forced gestures, to justify each one not being more expressive with him.

Those who played nervously commented on the progress of the game; The two peons raised their voices, feigning an argument that did not exist and thus each and every one ignored Frank, who, standing in the center of the establishment, did not know what attitude to take.

The situation was so violent that he wanted to grab each of the ears and shake them like rebellious rabbits, and then apply a resounding blow behind the ear appendages.

Calmly he went to the counter, and placing himself in front of the owner, he exclaimed:

"Good evening, Oliver. What's going on here? Is there sick, or is it that people have lost the sense of education?

Oliver, a little confused, replied:

"Hi Frank. No ... There is no sick person ... otherwise ... I don't know ... People have been a bit distracted for a long time. There are many concerns ...

And very little sense of decency. Give me a glass of whiskey.

Oliver rushed to serve him while looking seriously at him from the corner of his eye. You could tell that he too was worried and prey to the same nervousness that plagued everyone.

Frank took the glass, took it with his right hand, turned his back to the counter, leaning against the complacent, and with the heel of his high boot resting on the footing bar, he wandered his questioning gaze around the place.

His sharp eyes observed the confusion that dominated everyone. Each one adopted a posture that placed him in such a way that he did not have to confront him and whoever could not achieve this had his head bent over the cards or glasses and his eyes peeked, pretending to observe without being observed.

Frank, smiling enigmatically, examined one by one in silence. It seemed as if he was trying to read in their gestures and postures the amount of contempt they felt for him and perhaps the reason that forced them to show it in that cowardly way.

He did not know the reason, although he was suspecting that it lay in Hamson's influence and perhaps in his theories for wanting to involve him in the tragic assault on the Missouri stagecoach, but he would have been more grateful for a face attack, the rudeness of a virile accusation, erroneous or true, that that indecorous and lack of all manhood.

Suddenly he felt frizzy. It was not they but he who was being in a slighted situation, and seized with a fit of rage, he took hold of the glass that he held with his sinewy fingers and smashed it in anger against the ground while shouting:

"Well, gentlemen, I am waiting for an explanation!

A deathly silence followed the muffled crash of the glass against the platform of the floor. The game was cut off, the drinkers left their glasses gently on the table tops so as not to produce noise, and dozens of eyes, in which amazement was reflected, looked at each other in a questioning way, avoiding tripping over Frank's fiery and fiery.

The latter, observing that no one answered his question, advanced coldly saying:

"I am waiting for an answer, gentlemen.

James Lawson, the owner of a sawmill, perhaps the rudest and least timid of all, believed himself to be more directly alluded to when he observed that Frank's eyes, turning, were fixed on him, and rising, he exclaimed:

"You mean something specific, Frank?

He smiled evasively and replied:

"Well, thank God there is even one who proves to be less of a coward than the others. Indeed, Mr. Lawson, I am referring to something specific: I have been away from here for three years; I left in frank friendship with everyone or almost everyone present, and now, when I return and meet you again, instead of finding that warmth of friendship that I left when I left, I find that I have been greeted as if by commitment and even with disgust. I think I have the right to ask them why, even if I don't care why later.

Lawson, in an elusive way, replied:

"I don't think you can expect people to maintain an eternal friendship when they consider that it is not convenient for them to do so.

"Indeed, I neither pretend nor desire it, when it is not born from the heart, but I do feel obliged to ask the one who until yesterday was my friend, why he has stopped being a friend when there was no reason for it.

"Do you think there wasn't? Frank, you know us all. Although at this moment I speak for myself, I believe I interpret the feelings of others. We have always been cordial in our friendships, but when someone stopped deserving it, we have not tried to shoot it off. Just stopping cultivating it is enough. You believe that there is no reason and we believe that there is ... at least until you make us fall from the error.

"When you left there were specific accusations against you. Perhaps they were not so specific that they deserved to mobilize all the sheriffs of the West to bring you here to answer for them, but you were very questioned, and now, when you return after time, not only do you not come to erase that, but you see yourself mixed In a matter as dark as that.

«There is no evidence against you in this one either, but neither have you clarified like sunlight that there can be no suspicion. Everyone has their susceptibility and when they believe that a person does not meet the moral conditions that they consider fair to cultivate their friendship, they leave them and ... that's all.

There was a moment of tremendous anticipation among the establishment regulars as they heard the old sawyer express himself with that rude but sensible firmness against which there was no room for manifestations of violence.

Frank listened to him through clenched teeth, his eyes fixed on hers. He was receiving the bitter spoonful with as much phlegm as possible, although in his chest a blaze of rage burned, not against the interlocutor, but against the one who had lit the firebrand of distrust and contempt.

When Lawson finished speaking, Frank calmly replied:

"Thank you very much for your frankness, Mr. Lawson. I want to admit the reasons you give me to justify your attitude, which is that of everyone present and perhaps that of those who are not. Well, I cannot oppose any reason for the moment, but you forget that my enemy has not been able to oppose, despite his old hatred, anything that can satisfy his revenge and lead you to think so. I know where the blow comes from and I fit it like a perfect fighter that I am.

«I cannot blame you for your childish credulity and even more so because, forgetting my history and that of my family, you have believed me capable of committing ignoble actions and come to present myself with cynicism in front of you. There their consciences at the time of realizing, mutual account of their mistakes. For my part, I will only say that I do not take into consideration that undeserved contempt. There are many days of struggle left, many things to clarify and many things to know, but I will tell you that the day things become clear and they will be clarified because I am the first to have an interest in it, do not come to apologize to me. By Judas, don't do it, because the first one who comes to do it, I'll put five bullets into him for being stupid!

«I am glad that this situation has occurred, because it saves me new blushes that I do not know how I would be able to fit, but hear this: I have come to fight and I will fight. You have allowed yourself to be dominated by whoever is exploiting you and imposing your criteria and the day will come when you will realize your sheep behavior. I am a free man who does not admit tutelage and I will shake them off. We are going to have fun times in this town and I will not be the least to laugh when they occur. Thank you very much, Mr. Lawson, for your honesty.

"We will have the opportunity to discuss the subject again, but when I am the one who has to humiliate them, how they have tried to humiliate me, laughing at them more tragic and above all more real things than those stupid accusations.

He turned to the counter, tossed a few coins on the tin, and turning around, prepared to leave the bar followed uneasily by the fleeing glances of everyone present.

The young man's words had left them confused and embarrassed. There was restraint and acceptance in them, but also covert firmness and aggressiveness, something like a hidden fiber of confidence and self-assurance that made him despise the unconfirmed rumors that had been attributed to him.

For a moment, they all looked at each other confused, as if wondering if they had really been right to behave like this with him or if, on the contrary, they had committed one of the greatest and most unforgivable vileities of his life.

But there was no longer a remedy. The friendship had been broken and according to Frank's warning, he had no possible composure.

By the time Frank reached the doorway, a figure interposed, forcing him to take a few steps back. It was Dennis, and Frank, despite his anger that worried him, discovered to the point that he was drunk.

Dennis wasn't exactly intoxicated, but he was under the excitement of alcohol.

Hamson's harsh words, Sylvia's cold and a little contemptuous attitude and a little awareness of knowing that he was in a false position after the incident at the Post Office, forced him to erase the outrage suffered and, as he knew, less risky and determined than his rival, he chose to increase his value in the false and ephemeral courage that alcohol lends.

Dennis had drunk more than necessary in some of the local taverns he had been looking for Frank, and as he filled his stomach with alcohol, his head filled with aggressive vapors and his words took on tones of violence and aggressiveness.

Wherever he passed he bragged that he had been looking for Frank all afternoon to undo him with his fists, until someone who had seen the young man enter Oliver's bar, told him:

"If you really want to meet him, you don't need to run long. I saw him walk into Kukon's bar a while ago. You will surely find it there.

"Thank you," Dennis mumbled. I'm going to see if it's true or if he knows I'm looking for him and he's hidden in a hole like ants.

And with a hesitant step, he went to the bar.

Frank, seeing him, guessed that he was coming with a desire for revenge and smiled expressively. He couldn't have chosen a more propitious time for it, given his state of mind.

Impassive, she stared at him, and Dennis, taking a step forward, exclaimed hoarsely:

"What's wrong with you, Frank? You seem to look at me as if you are afraid of me. No doubt you think that now you will not be able to hit me off guard like the other night and you are not sure of being as successful as then.

They all looked at Dennis in amazement. They did not think of him as a fighting man, much less to allow themselves to challenge Frank, and a feeling of morbid curiosity washed over them.

Frank contemptuously replied:

"Listen, Dennis. I am a man who has not been scared by anyone, least of all a useless and lanky guy like you. I understand that alcohol is making you brave and I would feel that people commented that I had taken advantage of your inferiority to give you severe punishment.

«If you are really anxious for revenge, and I take care of it, because you should not have been very graceful in front of that Hamson toad and less in front of Sylvia, sleep the drunkenness and when you are in your right mind and measure your value without false boasting, you will have me at your disposal for revenge.

Dennis laughed hoarsely, saying:

"That smells scary to me, Frank! The other day I was serene as you say and you wasted no time talking. You got ahead of yourself just in case. I do not deny that I have had a few drinks, but it was not to take courage, but to not get bored trying to find you in vain.

Frank, impatient, replied:

"Okay, I wanted to save everyone's eyes from anyone falsely accusing me again. If you think you are fit to fight, I am at your service.

"So falsely, huh?" Dennis grumbled, grinning stupidly. Do you mean to deny that you were in tandem with your partner and that you shared Hamson's loot? And do you think people ...?

Frank, exasperated by the repetition in accusing him of that robbery in which he had not taken any part, could not contain the impulse of rage that dominated him and stretching his fist in a fulminating way, he applied it on the still delicate mouth of Dennis, forcing him to emit a terrible scream of pain.

"Stupid carrion! Son of a wolf! "Roared Frank." Rectify that slander you're spouting right now, or by Judas I swear I'll beat your mouth out! Do it, Dennis, do it or I'll destroy you! '

Dennis, enraged by the blow received and encouraged by the stubbornness of alcohol, raised his hand to his mouth, drawing it back full of blood and his eyes reddish with anger, he blurted out:

"I'm not rectifying anything, damn your heart, you filthy highwayman! Hit if you can, but I'll undo you forever and you'll never be my nightmare again. You have come to steal Sylvia from me and you won't make it.

Dennis, exalted, moved, looking for a way to apply his fist to Frank's face, but Frank, cold and serene, easily dodged him and returned the blows in cash, roaring:

"Rectify, Dennis, rectify or I'll blow your mouth off! ...

Dennis was taking the blows to his teeth, enduring the pain of the terrible fists, and he was slapping furiously trying to reply properly, while grunting:

"No! ... I do not rectify! Gunman! Robber!...

At each insult, Frank, more out of his mind, exerted his terrible blows and the face of his rival was something he imposed, without Dennis seeming to notice the pain.

Suddenly, feeling struck in the chest, he bent forward roaring like a tiger and painfully leaned back for a moment indecisive, with reddish eyes and two terrible purple circles around them, then, his right hand sank into In his jacket pocket and in his hand, a huge knife appeared, glinting sinisterly for a moment, then searching fiercely for Frank's chest, without Dennis, as he began the mortal journey, taking care of the brutal blows he received.

Frank, realizing the terrible danger he was in, jumped back abruptly avoiding the mortal trip, being about to slip, but with a powerful sprain he straightened himself stretching his arm.

His agility managed to grab hold of Dennis's fiercely wielding knife, and using his cultivated forces, he not only parried the blow, but twisted Dennis's arm in such a way that the farmer bent down to his knees writhing like a vine shoot.

Frank continued to squeeze him to the ground, and when he had him held down defenselessly, he flexed his arm and slowly, relishing the hideous feat, began to bend Dennis's arm until the point of the knife threatened his throat.

A collective scream of horror rose from the throats of everyone present. They understood that Frank had been challenged by Dennis and that Dennis had deviously wielded the knife, avoiding all sporting rules in the fight, but his physical inferiority was so manifest that that end, more than the result of an effort in the fight, was a cold blooded murder.

It was Lawson who, rising impetuously, roared:

"Frank, no, by hell! That is not noble!

Frank hesitated for a moment; He looked at Lawson in a special way and squeezing Dennis's forearm furiously, forced him to drop the knife.

He took it with the opposite hand and getting up, crossed his arms in front of his enemy, who, half destroyed, remained on the ground without the strength to get up.

Then, in a dismissive tone, he exclaimed:

"Dennis, you are an idiot who thinks by dictation. I must have killed you for an imbecile and if I haven't, it's because I know that it wasn't you, but the whiskey that launched you to challenge me. Go away, go away and don't ever put yourself in front of me again, if you don't want me to really undo you.

"Someday we will talk about these insults and both you and that pig Hamson will pay me the damage you are trying to do to me.

Dennis, unconsciously, got up, and more humiliated than ever, crawled towards the door disappearing from the bar.

Frank put the knife away and, glaring at the customers, was also absent. He had given them proof of his chivalry by not killing Dennis as was his right. Nothing mattered to him what they thought of his action.

It is true that in the paroxysm of fury he had been on the point of not stopping when he bent the arm of his rival, but a feeling of nobility had restrained him.

One thing served as a palliative to the fury. Suppose the vinegar gesture that Hamson would make when he found out the end of the adventure and the bitterness and spite that Sylvia would suffer when she knew the new failure of her stupid fiancé.

But this, being something, did not quite satisfy Frank. His self-esteem, his dignity and his honesty were wounded and in question. Clearly they had made it known to him at the bar and although his conscience was clear, he could not avoid the bitterness of knowing himself so unjustly accused of Hamson's viciousness and hatred.

But each one would have their turn. Dennis had already had part of it, then it would be the turn of the godly banker whom he had to humiliate much lower than he had tried to humiliate him, and then ...

He did not feel hatred towards Sylvia, but rather spite for her volubility, but he did feel the urge to teach her a profound lesson so that she would realize that in her foolish vanity, she had chosen the worst, disdaining, not only her happiness, but also feeling protected. for a whole and honest man as he was.

CHAPTER VII

THE SURPRISE OF THE RESCUE

At night, Frank couldn't get to sleep. He was tormented by the violence of the situation and wondered what he could try to find a solution to it. Suddenly the episode of the outlaw's flight came to his mind. The leather bag split by the strap sinking into the muddy Missouri stream flowered again in his imagination, and although he was not very confident in his idea, he planned to go that next morning to the river and dive to the bottom in the mad hope of being able to locate The bag.

She shouldn't have too much confidence in finding him. The river, dragging the spring alluvium, carried a lot of water those days and it could have dragged it God knew where.

It all depended on his weight. If most of the money consisted of paper, the sack could not have resisted the force of the water, letting itself be dragged like a log; but if the majority of the content was made up of gold, perhaps its excessive weight would have caused it to sink into the silt of the river, where with more or less patience it could be located.

He was angered by the idea that he was precisely the one who was returning the money to Hamson. Against all that he argued, the loss should revert to him, but in the absence of better proof for his innocence, that could free him from the unjust baldness that weighed on him.

As soon as dawn broke, he mounted his horse, and without being observed, he headed for the river. A morning bath wouldn't hurt, even if he couldn't find what he was looking for.

When he finally reached the shore of the Missouri, he stopped studying the terrain. He must not get disoriented, looking for the closest place where the robber fled, or else he would waste his time pitifully.

At last he remembered a detail that was going to guide him for sure. When the black horse was steadying its legs on the soft shore, Frank had unconsciously noticed a tree with twisted branches, the trunk of which, very low, split at about five feet, forming two forked arms that they rose straight.

He soon discovered the tree, and rejoicing, he stripped off his clothes and jumped into the water.

The current was not very powerful. The Missouri had turbulent times and times when it was harmless and although it was not yet midsummer that its current half dried up, the flow of water was not to scare a swimmer like him.

The only thing that bothered him was having to swallow that dirty and muddy liquid that dragged the earth torn from the banks and the grasses and branches that fell into the stream in its bosom, but he could not avoid it, and without hesitation, he made up his mind.

He swam to the opposite shore and when he found himself in front of the tree, he sank gracefully, searching for the bottom. In that part he found him barely six feet away, and moving like a fish, he plunged his hands into the mud, feeling anxiously for the leather sack.

When his contracted lungs could not take it any longer, he would rise to the surface with a heel to take a breath and again he plunged with determination, willing not to give up on his project until he was convinced that, in fact, the bag could not be in a space of three or four meters in relation to the place where he saw him fall. It was stubborn work that consumed half an hour of time. Every couple of minutes he would come out of the water puffing like a seal, his face and hands muddy, but as soon as his lungs regained normalcy, he once again threw himself to the bottom willing not to be defeated by the refusal.

Until, finally, when despair was taking hold of him and he was ready to give up the exhausting task, his hands stumbled on an object, which he grasped with eagerness, for the air was already running out, and with a strong blow, rose.

A cry of triumph escaped from his chest as he recognized the coveted sack among the layer of mud that covered him, and swimming with it, he gained the shore where he had left his horse, already quite well from his twisted leg.

He put it on the ground, sat in the sun, gasping for air, and when he felt somewhat rested, he dipped the bag into the stream until it was clean of all the filth that disfigured it.

Then, he examined him carefully. The jacket with the initials WM and the name "Banco Ganadero Nirvay" left no room for doubt.

The mouth was hermetically closed with a fine but resistant wire and the ends of the wire appeared lost inside a crushed lead seal, which prevented any violation of the contents.

As for the weight, although it was not excessive, it was quite heavy. It had to contain at least three or four thousand dollars in gold and the rest in paper.

Frank was pleased with the find and wondered what to do with the bag.

Now he was sorry that he had not declared the detail when the sheriff questioned him. It had been kept as a personal secret, and if he returned it now, what comments might the return lead to?

Possibly they would judge that he had repented after the robbery and that, at the cost of returning the bag and its contents, he tried to avoid that, later investigations, they could accuse him more fully and take him to jail, and who knew if he was hanged.

His situation was worse now than before. He had the proof of the crime, it was he who only knew it and had the stolen amount in his possession.

A shadow of doubt covered his eyes. He was wondering if it wasn't better to dip the sack back into the current, not on the shore, but in the center, where no one could find him. It would be capital that would be lost forever, but it would not serve to further complicate his already complicated situation.

After a moment of agonizing uncertainty, he chose to get rid of that sack that burned his fingers like a burning ember. It was better to leave things as they were and not complicate them on your own.

If the outlaw had lost his sack, too bad for him ... but why, if he realized the loss, hadn't he tried what he had and had come back looking for it?

Since he was exposing himself to so much for the theft of the damn sack, the least he could have tried was his ransom. This just complicated his conflicting thoughts.

There were details that did not rhyme with each other and it was not explained why.

The mind of the undesirables was not very subtle for lack of education and exercise.

They committed a crime out of greed or necessity and no detail or danger stopped them that they did not believe they were in a position to go back with a revolver in their hand, and if so, it was not explained that they had not returned in search of the treasure, although perhaps not He would have done so for fear that his pursuer, observing that the sack had fallen into the water, would try to use it as bait against him if he returned to look for him.

He was determined to return it to the river, when when he took it low in his hands, he put pressure on it and he was suspended for a moment. Touch had told him something very vague, but just enough to stop the action.

What had it been? Frank concentrated on himself and pressed again to clarify what it was about.

He soon realized it. Above the body, he had imprisoned something hard "undoubtedly the cartridges of gold coins", but the touch rebelled to accept it. The shape of those cartridges did not seem the usual one in such a class of coins.

Feverishly he continued to feel in all directions, and the more he fumbled with the hard objects that the mysterious sack contained, the more convinced he was that they were not packed cartridges of coins, not even loose change. It was something different that he could not analyze.

And a subtle suspicion replaced the doubt. It was being said that there were many strange details that surrounded that event and there he was shown one that in his opinion increased the enigma of what happened.

With his impetuousness, he reached for the knife and applied it to the leather to tear it. He needed to get out of doubt and he was not a man who had the nerves to leave a situation that he could clarify a mystery.

But the momentum gave way to a call from common sense. The moment he opened the sack on his own account and without witnesses, nothing that might happen later had any value. Everything could be the product of his inventiveness and it was not something that could suit him.

The best measure was to gallop in search of Lang, give him an account of everything and put the sack in his hands, taking him as a witness to open it.

Perhaps the sheriff would refuse to do so, in which case he would not be squeamish and slash him in front of him and then invoke his testimony.

Without further hesitation, he dressed, mounted his horse, and hiding the sack, he went to the village.

When he arrived at Lang's offices, Lang was busy reviewing various communications received from sheriffs in the towns that extended to both divisions. No one had seen any stranger riding a black horse, since it was not easy for them to see him if he had crossed that way.

Upon discovering Frank with a regular lump hiding him under his jacket, he asked:

What is it, Frank? What the hell are you hiding under your jacket with so much mystery?

"Well ... I don't know how to qualify it, but you will immediately judge when I tell you something that the other day I kept exclusively because I thought it was a trivial thing that would seem like something from a novel to tell. You will remember that I was going to try to find proof in my favor. Well, I have found it and I am coming to bring it to you.

And opening his jacket, he showed the sheriff's surprised eyes the leather jacket.

When Lang realized what it was all about, he exclaimed:

"For a hundred thousand heck, Frank! Where did you have that hidden?

Frank, smiling, replied:

"Don't look at me like that, Lang. He didn't have it hidden anywhere. I came from rescuing him from where he fell and it took me half an hour to swallow some mud to find him.

And, succinctly, he told her the detail of the loss of the leather jacket that had fallen silent, almost certain that the current had carried it away.

The sheriff took the sack and carefully examined the strap. Indeed, it was split in a peculiar way and he did not hesitate to admit that the bullet could have split the leather.

"Well, boy" he said "this may be decisive for you ... I do not deny that someone will question the veracity of the finding, it is a bit fantastic, but the reality is that Hamson recovers his fifty thousand dollars although with it , poor Jasper doesn't come back to life.

"What's your idea?" Asked Frank.

"Call Hamson, hand him the sack, and tell him how he was rescued by you.

"I refuse at all," replied the young man firmly. Hamson will not see this sack ... at least until we have opened and examined its contents.

"Are you crazy?" Asked the sheriff. We are not the one to do that. The bag has the seal intact and thus must be returned to its owner.

"Forcing him to open it in his presence?

"Why, if you don't want to? As soon as you recognize the bag as yours and are satisfied also acknowledging that it appears intact, we do not have to force you to show us the contents. That is up to him and his business.

"Do you think so? Well, not me.

" Because it causes?

"For a very simple one. Have you ever had cartridges of gold coins in your hands?

"Not many, but yes sometimes. I was a ranch foreman and handled a lot of money on behalf of my employer.

"So you have to recognize by touch what a coin cartridge is and what it is not.

"Naturally.

"Well, please feel carefully for those hard objects that the bag contains and tell me if you think they could be cartridges of coins.

The intrigued sheriff, obeyed the suggestion of the young man and after palpating and probing countless times on the leather, he murmured softly:

"By the heck you're making me wonder, Frank! No, I can't say they look like coin cartridges to me!

"Well, if they really aren't, what the hell is in this damn sack?

"I don't know, Frank... I swear I'm disoriented.

"Not me, although I might be smart. Listen to this; Hamson has trumpeted that the sack contained fifty thousand dollars in gold and paper, if it does not contain them, what happens?

" Hell's Bells! Where are you going to stop?

"Simply, because then it is a crime of fraud.

"For a hundred thousand pairs of cow horns, Frank! Do you want to drive me crazy?

"Not. I want to clarify things. Either it contains what Hamson has stated, or it does not. If it is gold, other than in nuggets, it cannot be admitted that it is otherwise and if it is not ... then the possibilities that open up to you as sheriff are enormous, because in such a case, it is not only about a crime of fraud, but of something more tragic.

"I do not understand.

"You will understand me. If the bag arrived at a destination containing something that is not declared, someone had to take the blame for a change and ... it could not be more than poor Jasper and if you did not want to run the risk that the bag would arrive with what it contains, to avoid many complications, in that case ... the interested party himself knows much more than I do about the assault on the stagecoach and the death of Jasper.

«For this reason, I did not want to touch the bag but it was in front of you and that is why I refuse to have it returned unopened. Me and with you, I need to know exactly what it contains.

"We can force him to open it in our presence ... I will force him.

"And you might spoil it all. He will do it and say that this bag is not the one he sent, that someone seized a bag from the Bank and changed it. Furthermore, when it comes to me, he is capable of affirming that I was the author of the heavy joke and nothing we can prove to him that it is illegal.

"But, Frank... what interest would he have in doing such a thing? He is responsible for the loss of money and admitting that Hamson intended to commit a scam, he committed it against himself, who will be the one who has to pay the lost.

" You believe? Wait a few hours or a few days and you will see how this does not happen. He intends to charge the loss on the depositories and that amount will have been pocketed.

"Don't talk nonsense! Hamson is rich enough not to commit this dangerous little thing.

"Well, wait, I say. When the bank was robbed, you will remember that you loaded what should have been stolen from the depositories. Interest was reduced to cover the loss.

"Devil, it's true! I did not remember it.

And now he will pretend to do the same.

"But that is unheard of for a wealthy man!

"You don't know the truth of your money. You can have it and the ambition to lose you, you can pretend you have it and be drowned. You know you speculate.

He longs to be a millionaire, because his golden dream is to be a senator. God knows of the means that it tries to use to be it.

But this is very serious. There is a death involved.

"Because there is, I am opposed to your idea.

"What do you propose then?

"Open the bag and check what it contains.

"Well. Let's admit that it is not what he said. What will happen next?

"Nothing at the moment. You and I are going to be the only ones who know what the sack contains. He is smart and will know how to avoid danger, even if there is some doubt floating around.

"You're building on sand, Frank.

"No, and I beg you to wait a bit. I want to see where it breathes. I am sure he will try to charge the loss on the depositories.

"It would not be legal or logical.

"But he is the master and he will threaten them. If it goes well, he'll pocket the money, and then maybe it's time to bring up the contents of the bag.

"It's hard for me to accept it.

"Not me. I think the time has come to do some research on Hamson's financial activities. If he has suffered any failure, put in the trigger will commit another new scoundrel.

"What can you do?

"I don't know, but I promise to be vigilant. Hamson is my prey and I am the owl who will destroy him.

"But Jasper's death remains ...

"All the more reason to wait. If he manages to slip away from this accusation, that wretch will be without revenge. Trust me, Lang, I don't ask for fantasies like Hamson asked about me. I ask for realities.

"Well, I'm going to wait a little while, not long. I will keep this bag where no one will see if your suspicions are really true. Let's see it.

Frank, with the knife, tore the leather and dumped the contents on the table. They both looked at each other in amazement.

They found chunks of lead filed down to somewhat simulate the shape of coin cartridges.

They were wrapped in pieces of paper torn from some illustrated magazines from the East, magazines that no one in the town received and that only a wealthy and refined person could receive.

But there was still more; one of the rough ingots was wrapped in a piece of white paper. Frank slipped the lead off and showed the pristine piece of paper. This one appeared torn at the head, no doubt to eliminate something written or printed on it, but cut abruptly, the tear came out imperfect and a piece of what was suppressed or tried to suppress, remained in the mutilated sheet. Frank showed it to him triumphantly saying:

"Look at those edges, they are lower pieces of letters and if you look for some form of the Bank and compare it, you will see that they correspond to the lower part of the letterhead.

Lang nodded. Frank's intuition was revealing many things to him that he had never imagined.

"You're right, boy, and I'm getting convinced that Hamson is a rogue. I will put the sack away and we will wait for new developments.

Thank you, Lang. I am glad that you have been a sensible man who has not been suggested by the influence of that rogue. Not all sheriffs know how to maintain their prestige and authority. If he threatens to make you substitute, laugh at him. You are assured of re-election for a long time.

And radiant with joy at the discoveries made, he left the offices ready to launch himself into the fight. He thought he knew Hamson and knew that when an idea took hold in his brain, he was unable to give it up, for good or bad.

Frank was sure that the stagecoach robbery had been planned to make the leather jacket disappear, the only way to erase all vestige of his skillful feat, but who had committed the robbery?

The young man was currently unaware of the elements that Hamson could use for his business. Formerly, he had unscrupulous men on the ranch, such as the one who had given himself to affirm that he had recognized him in that simulated cattle rustling to lose him, but having got rid of the ranch, he did not know who could have been the one to take charge of such a dirty task .

Of course, he assumed that the person existed. He did not believe Hamson capable of performing it in person and the important thing was to monitor him until he found someone suspicious who was in relation to him.

This was not considered easy at the moment. Hamson had to be very alert after what had happened. His intention of taking advantage of Frank's arrival to blame him, if he had not entirely failed, it had not curdled as he wished to shake off all possible suspicions and he would remain alert so as not to commit any slip that could be fatal to him.

The undoubted thing was, that whoever had acted in his name should be protected and hidden by him in a safe place and had to be discovered, as well as the famous black horse that served to help the robber to slip away.

And with a head full of projects, he decided to wait for the new activities of his enemy.

$$\star\ \star\ \star$$

Frank's suspicions were soon confirmed as to Hamson's intentions to shake off the danger of having to pay for the mock robbery himself.

The next morning, a notice signed by Hamson appeared on the door of the Bank in which he summoned all the depositors of money in the Bank for the following day, to discuss a matter of utmost importance to them.

The people, a bit candid, assumed that the former rancher summoned them to give them an official account of the event and to, in a presumptuous trait, inform them that, not being able to place the responsibility of the disappearance on anyone affected by the Bank, he accepted the loss on his own Although he might be begging for help to cover the deficit.

Frank read the notice as he passed and when he returned home, he said to his father:

"I hope that you will allow me to come on your behalf to that meeting. I will be thankful.

"What do you propose?" Asked his father uneasily.

"Nothing violent, don't be alarmed. I intend to defend your money and that of everyone in the town, even if they don't deserve it. I have the evidence that Hamson will try to bear the loss and I am willing not to consent to it.

Old Neil agreed, but Frank was careful not to tell his rot what he had discovered. He understood that the fewer they were in the secret the better and he would have time to launch the news with the same force that could launch a charge of dynamite.

And with full control of his nerves, he waited for the arrival of the next day to attend the meeting.

CHAPTER VIII

FRANK GOES ON THE COUNTER ATTACK

It would be ten in the morning the next day when fifty landowners, industrialists, ranchers and merchants of Nirvay and its surroundings were gathered in the spacious hall of the Bank, equipped by its employees for such an important meeting.

Frank's presence was greeted with coldness and even with disguised contempt, but the young man, without appreciating those hostile demonstrations, found a seat in the last chairs against the wall and waited for the meeting to begin.

Her keen eyes scanned the crowd, discovering the sheriff and Dennis's father between them, but not Dennis, who should not be in a physical position to appear publicly.

A quarter of an hour later, Hamson appeared elegantly dressed, in his long black frock coat, his fancy waistcoat full of gaudy embroidery, his tube-shaped suede trousers, and his tall leather boots with spurs.

It was a half hero, half cowboy outfit that he had adopted for his personal use.

He carried a large wallet under his arm, and after greeting the crowd gravely, he positioned himself behind a small table set to one side in front of the rows of benches destined for depositors.

Before speaking, he examined the faces of his clients and a deep wrinkle furrowed his forehead when he discovered Frank's figure in the background. He was smiling slightly and Hamson was not amused by either his presence or that threatening smile.

Hamson cleared his throat a little before deciding to speak and finally, in an affected tone, said:

"My dear friends, I am the first to regret the reason that compelled me to call this meeting, but events compel me to do so. My pleasure would have been to call you to tell you something pleasant that perhaps one day not far away I can communicate to you, but for now, the reason is unpleasant and painful.

«You know how I know what has happened recently with the Missouri stagecoach. Men without scruples or conscience "and when he said it he looked boldly at Frank" have not hesitated to shed innocent blood, just to appropriately without risk of foreign quantities that today endanger the economy of many of you.

«Urgent and lawful needs of the Bank forced me to entrust the driver of the stagecoach with a leather sack with fifty thousand dollars, for a transfer that inescapably had to be made to Marsland, and by means that I do not know, someone knew or suspected of this shipment and he stormed the stagecoach, appropriating that important sum. I have nothing to reproach myself for.

«The operation was lawful. The precautions I took are exquisite. I personally kept the money in the sack, sealed it and gave it to the head of the Casa de Postas and took care to see it in the stagecoach after making sure of the honesty of the mayoral. It was all I could do and I did. The rest has been the work of luck or God knows what.

"The fact itself is that the common fund has suffered such a decline that is not attributable to me. As the Bank does not have its own capital, but the existing capital is yours, being yours, the loss has to revert to you.

A murmur of discontent rumored through the hall. Hamson, uneasy, silenced with a gesture saying:

"I understand that this is painful for you, but it is also painful for me that I want to unite my luck with yours, bearing that loss in a prudent proportion. Nobody is going to reduce the capital deposited in my Bank. I do not want the theft to cause you that loss, but there is a need to find a formula that will help make up for that deficit and I have come to offer you the formula.

«I have my capital, which is not large, also noted in my checking account books and therefore, the loss will also affect me and what I propose is to suspend the payment of interest for a limited time that allows the reversal and that even those who can, increase deposits with new contributions that will allow the deficit to be settled in a short time.

This is not loss in itself. Your money will always be guaranteed by my honor, and the waiver of a small interest is not a loss, since it does not diminish the money you have entrusted to me.

"Here there are ranchers and landowners who have deposits in banks in the region. Why should they not patriotically help their own, investing in it the money deposited in others to increase the volume and help the gap to be quickly wiped away?

This will be a temporary thing. On the other hand, although I should not speak and although I allow myself to do it in a veiled way, I will anticipate that thanks to my efforts, very shortly I will be able to give you sensational news, which will not only make you happy, but will increase the value of everything you have. It will be something great and beneficial and I am sorry that I do not say more, because I have already said too much. It is necessary to guard against the thieves of initiatives, as against the robbers of stagecoaches.

«I hope that men like Jim Powell, who one day soon will be a relative of mine, industrialists like James Lawson, ranchers like Ray Prince and others here present, will support my initiative and reinforce the capital of our Bank, bridging this pothole without suffering any loss in your capital.

«Fifty thousand dollars are quickly recovered with an austere regime in the administration and an increase in cash of about one hundred thousand dollars that allow the Bank to maneuver with ease in loans, mortgages and advances, on solid collateral, with an interest that compensates us for this stupid loss.

«I await the opinion of those who can and should do so to know what to expect.

Before anyone had time to speak, Frank got up, requesting to do so.

Hamson, furious, replied:

"You have no interests in this Bank. Your presence here is not only hateful, but untimely.

"One moment. I represent my father; my father has his money deposited here and I must watch over his money. I have a perfect right to intervene on your behalf.

Hamson bit his lip, and with a grunt, sat up.

Frank, looking at the audience who were looking at him curiously, began by saying:

"As for my father, not only will he not contribute a single penny to add to the deposits, but he does not admit the loss of legal interest.

Hamson stood up in a basilisk, protesting loudly, but Frank, cool and collected, replied:

"Please let me speak. You have done it and you have been listened to, I have that right.

Soon, it found an echo in the audience. He was defending everyone's money and they liked his trait.

Frank added:

"We do not know nor do we want to know about the internal regime of your Bank. You, on your own initiative, sent that money without guarantees and without asking anyone for an opinion and you are only responsible for its loss. To load it on us, it was necessary for the depositaries to give their opinion in the administrative process and that the way to send the money had been submitted to them for approval. So yes, because we would all have been responsible for the recklessness.

«A quantity like this is sent with more guarantees. People are collected to guard the deposit and defend it, and they do not give themselves over to a poor old man who, no matter how brave he might have been, could do nothing against surprise.

"Of which you should know a lot" said Hamson.

Let's say I know everything. That says nothing, because if those stupid insinuations could have value, I would pay with my neck for the crime of having committed it, but none of these gentlemen had to lose a penny since the fault of the loss was theirs.

Hamson, like a cornered beast, screamed:

"I hope that these gentlemen will not have an opinion like you because, if so, they would not only endanger the life of the Bank, but also the money deposited.

"We'll talk about that, Mr. Hamson. You have assured that the Bank does not have capital. Where, then, does the interest you pay come from? Of the movement of that capital in loans, mortgages, purchases and sales, who knows the volume and performance of the application of that money? No one.

" The board of directors!

"The Council knows nothing. They are men of good faith, who do not know arithmetic and trust your words and the sheer volume of papers that you present to them.

«I know for sure, and I, who believe I have the right to do so, demand that in order to check if there is indeed a danger of bankruptcy, if there is no interest and if the help that you are requesting is needed, a commission of knowledgeable men be appointed to review all the accounts, balance sheets and documents of the life of the Bank, to give an opinion.

Hamson put his hand to his chest as if he had been hit with a sledgehammer. That was something that hurt him deeply, and like a beast, he roared:

" Never! I do not admit such an insult! I'm a man...

"A man like everyone else, or perhaps different from everyone," interrupted Frank, "and if you are so sure that what you have just told us is true and honest, not only should you not oppose, but you should be the first to provide those facilities. that will strengthen your situation and earn you that support that only with such an examination can be granted or not.

Frank's words raised a clamor of approval from the crowd. He was giving evidence of energy in front of the pernicious influence of the banker and although he was accusing him of nothing, it seemed as if a subtle suspicion was taking hold of them.

Hamson, livid and decomposed, roared:

" Never!! Those words, who have the least right to use them here, are such a manifest insult, such a disgusting humiliation, that I am going to reply to them as they deserve who will never be able to catch up with me in morality and honesty. I withdraw the request made and I wish nothing from anyone.

«I will lose those fifty thousand dollars from my private pocket and you will collect your interest. If they are so selfish, which is what they want, I have nothing to oppose. It seems to me that after this, there is no need for us to continue arguing.

An oh! of approval rose from all throats. Frank had won them a formidable battle that they were sure they would have lost without their intervention, but to their great amazement, Frank stood cool and collected, argued:

"It's the same, Mr. Hamson. I don't care if I put that money in or not. He has painted a disturbing picture regarding the future of the Bank and how I am not satisfied that this may be happening, I request that investigation.

"I said I don't admit it! I have a Board of Directors to which I will be accountable. Later...

"It's the same," Frank threatened. With and without the Council, I will ask on my own, paying whatever it costs if I am required to do so later, that the State verify a review of the accounts. When you have issued an opinion, you can continue to accuse me if you want, not only of robbery but of slanderer, it is the same to me. Since it has not been possible for you to have me convicted of the former, I want to give you the opportunity to have me convicted of the latter.

Hamson, furious, descended from the table trying to attack Frank.

He was looking for the revolver to fire on him, but the attendees of the tumultuous meeting cut him off, preventing him from doing so, while Frank, perfectly calm, smiled sinisterly, pondering the effect that his incisive statements had caused on the banker.

Hamson was dragged from the premises by force, but the rancher, flushed like sagebrush, roared:

"I'll kill you, Frank! You have been my black shadow for a long time and I am not a man who allows anyone to open pits for me on the way.

The meeting broke up in that spectacular fashion, and Frank was among the last to leave the bank.

At the door, the sheriff was waiting for him. Frank asked:

"What impression did you get from this, Lang?

"Do you want me to tell you sincerely? Well, Hamson is more afraid of an investigation at the Bank than to see his plan to seize those fifty thousand dollars frustrated.

"I was convinced of it. Now he cannot be let loose. Ruin is hanging over all the people in the village and it must be avoided.

" How?

"I dont know. I have not threatened you in vain. I will ask for that intervention, but I will let a few days pass to see how he reacts. In spite of everything, I do not want to jeopardize the money of all that credulous herd who have despised and insulted me so wickedly.

Lang worried, muttered:

"I'm not calm, Frank. I'm afraid, something strange on Hamson's part. I no longer believe him the man he seemed. You don't try such a desperate coup to grab fifty thousand dollars and then give it up. If you need them urgently, it is not possible for you to contribute them to the Bank; and if it does not contribute them ... what has he done with his personal fortune to need such tricks?

"I don't know and I would be glad to have some clue to know. In any case, I intend not to lose sight of him. I have to spy on him to see what his projects are. I suspect a tragic crisis is coming.

"Be careful. If he looks lost he is capable of shooting you.

"I will try not to give it a chance.

They parted. Frank went home to report to his father what had happened at the meeting, and Lang, very concerned, returned to his offices.

That same afternoon, something came up that Frank would not have suspected. It was partly a coincidence, but it could also have influenced chance so that the event did not have to be forced.

Frank had left to go to the village saddlery shop to have some stirrups fixed, when, crossing the main street, he faced Sylvia head-on. The girl walked serious and nervous and seemed to search for something with her eyes in an anguished way.

Frank, unable to avoid the encounter, tried to move away to the opposite side of the road, but when she saw him, she seemed to breathe with relief and crossing decisively, she motioned for him to stop.

He obeyed by stiffening, and the girl, in a pleading tone, exclaimed:

"Frank, I'd like to talk to you for a moment.

"No one is stopping you, Sylvia. I hear you.

"No ... I don't want it to be here so in public. Will you please meet me in half an hour at Willy's meadow?

" Why not? I will be all you want, but I am well mannered enough not to put a woman down. I'll wait for you there.

And slowly, he went to the place of the appointment. A meadow away from the town and protected by lush trees and a border hedge, which hid him even more from the view of those who came down to that place.

When Sylvia, all flushed, appeared in the meadow, Frank, unable to control the emotion caused by being able to speak alone with the woman who had constituted everything for him, exclaimed:

"Well, you will say what you have to ask me.

The girl, after a moment of nervous hesitation, exclaimed pleadingly:

"Frank, for all the saints, what have you set out to do?

"What do you mean, Sylvia?

"Your attitude towards us. What are you looking for and what do you want?

"I believe that nothing that is not lawful and legal. I should ask your father that question and ... yourself.

"I haven't done anything wrong to you, Frank.

"Not. Except that you treated me in an aggressive way when I told the truth of what happened with stagecoach.

She lowered her eyes in confusion, muttering:

"Maybe you're right. I don't remember exactly what I told you, but ... I was nervous about the blow suffered by my father ...

"And that's why you questioned my honesty, you who knew her better than anyone ...

"Frank ... I ... they had told me things that ... it is better not to repeat them ... you had not left a very clean poster when you were absent ... they accused you ...

"Your father only accused me and you know why. I was not the man you dreamed of. At that time he was a poor laborer on his ranch and although my father owned a fairly valuable warehouse and I could increase the business on any given day, all that was not enough.

«Your marrying a decent and honest man capable of the most audacious undertakings within the law, it was worthless. He needed a puppet for you, which wasn't even worth defending you, but that didn't matter; That you were at the mercy of the first one who wanted to offend you, had no value next to the handful of dollars that he could contribute to their businesses.

«And you ... you forgot our true friendship, our nascent love and proud of an education that is useless here because with it, within this town of honest but plain people, you are only an exotic thing to which you have to Put aside, you imbued yourself with your father's nonsense and surrendered to conceit and pride. It is very possible that you are very happy with Dennis, happier than with me, but, happy, in what way? That is what I would like to know.

She, who was listening to him troubled, murmured:

"I will not be happy with him, because we have broken our relations.

Frank's eyes widened at the statement and replied:

" What are you saying? Have you by now dared to provoke your father's anger by opposing his projects?

"I don't know or care. This is an intimate question. I wasn't very fond of Dennis, I admitted, because he seemed like a good boy and because someone, it had to be my husband one day, but the things that have happened have hurt me deeply. I did not take into account that you hit him the night of the post house. It was a surprise for him, but I did have to take what happened afterwards into account. He blazoned brave, promised to wash away the offense received and ... he sank deeper into the ridicule he was.

«Later ... I don't know ... someone told me that he had not fought with nobility ... and the man who is not noble to fight, is not noble at all ... But that is the least of it. The matters of my heart do not count, nor did I come to talk to you about them. You forced me and I think I was foolish to tell you. It came to something else that interests me more.

Frank got defensive. Things were happening that they considered very momentous for the future and he guessed that Sylvia, when he least expected it, was going to be an obstacle to his plans.

"What is it about?" He asked.

"Of my father. He's crazy, Frank. You have insulted and humiliated him to infinity. This morning you tried to sink his credit and good name, hinting at unsubstantiated accusations that have driven him crazy. Frank, by our old friendship! Do not put him through such distressing trances

"Has he hesitated to pass me off as other more terrible ones? He alone has been the cause of the whole town looking at me with suspicion and foolishly accusing me of an event of which I am clean and pure. I am a man who has never dyed his hands with innocent blood.

I'm not a murderer or a gunman like you and he called me. I handle the revolver, because it is the guarantee of my life like that of many in these climates, where the lives of men are not important, and I defend myself. I have fought many times, but always with nobility. Just yesterday, I was able to kill that puppet in legitimate defense and I didn't ... Why do I have to pay with a different currency than the one they use to pay me?

"On the other hand, I have done nothing but reject a suggestion from your father that harms my interests and ask him to give an account of how he handles our money. Is that an offense?

"For those who have a clear conscience ...

"He who has it, does not object, and is glad that his honesty shines. One thing is self-love and another is loyalty.

"Good, but he has offered to lose that money. What else do you want?

"Why is he going to lose it if he shouldn't? And if you must lose it, why are you opposed to showing your cards face up?

"Oh! ... You wouldn't understand, Frank. The matter is delicate. I talk to you as a friend ... My father has not taken anything from anyone, but at this moment, he has a colossal project in his hands that will be a pleasant surprise for the town.

Something very great and beneficial that he cannot account for, because if it were to fail it would destroy all a laborious work that will provide him with a fabulous profit and will make his Bank, the Banco del Poblado, one of the most important in the region.

"It is for this and nothing else that he is terrified of being involved in his business for the time being ... It is a matter of days. In a short time, he assures that the business will be finalized and there will no longer be any known danger. Frank, I'm not asking you not to defend yours ... I'm just asking you to delay that matter for a few days. Then you can do it and he is the first to be satisfied.

" You think so?

"I'm sure of it.

"Do you know what business it is?

"Not. He has not wanted to tell anyone ... not me, but he assures that it is a big thing.

"And what does he offer me in exchange for giving him those facilities?

"It is not him, but I who is asking you. He wouldn't ask you for anything even if he knew he was sinking forever.

"Well then, what do you offer?

" Nothing! I would be ashamed to know that you had bought or sold me the favor.

"It is very much in the Hamson family to ask and not to give. Pure selfishness that you cannot get rid of. Your father would not hesitate to hang me for a crime that I have not committed, but he would take advantage of my foolishness if I helped him with his plans ... And you, of his same caste, second him.

She bristled furiously:

" What do you know about that? I do not second. He is my father and I do what I can for him. You don't know this step of mine; if I knew, I would have the biggest upset of my life with him.

" Oh sure! I would accuse you of defending a gunman, a robber, a murderer and a thief, but if I give him facilities, he will take advantage of them and keep trying to lose me. Your father is an angel of finances.

"Stop it, Frank! I thought that in the name of our old friendship I could request that small favor of you, but I see that you are too spiteful to do so. It is the same, I will not insist more and I will accept what you or Fate want to bring me.

She, her eyes clouded by rebellious tears that struggled to appear, turned to leave, but Frank, seized with a mad desire for that love that had not yet died in his chest, ran towards her, gripped her by the arms and biting the words as he uttered them, he roared:

"I am going to do it, Sylvia, I am going to do it and the devil does not take me into account that with it I am failing my duty and one day you will understand that it was! I do it, because despite everything I still love you how I loved you when I left and because I had come back here pushed by that love that is stronger than my will. I do not want anything in return, not even a love that would only be a charity or a spite.

«I will do it out of my own vanity, to satisfy this foolish love that I still keep in my chest and that will be my ruin, but I will do it and when the things that have to happen have happened, then I will leave again and try to forget that it existed a woman who was once my glory and now only constitutes my hell.

And like a madman he fled from her side, leaving her stunned and confused.

CHAPTER IX

THE TEETH OF THE CEPO

An unprecedented fury seized Frank after the violent scene with Sylvia. She had been carried away by an irrepressible urge by making a foolish promise and now she had no choice but to be true to her word. Well ... I would fulfill it.

He would give Hamson a margin of time to fix his situation, a margin that he might use to look for money and offer an investigation a fictitious normality that would cease as soon as the impression passed, but he would not leave his hand and watch him at his best. minute details, to follow in his footsteps and try to find out what his machinations were.

In no mood to talk to anyone, the next day he mounted his horse, and letting the horse trot at will, he left the town up hills and clearings, crossing trails and streams and filtering through forests and cuttings without realizing it.

Suddenly, he realized that he had drifted too far from the village. At least ten miles to the east, on the opposite road to the one he had taken when he returned to town.

It was near Thedford, a town that also belonged to the route, a very short distance from the Missouri.

He was standing on the top of a hill in the pleasant shade of a group of trees that preserved him from the fierce morning sun, when, glancing at the path below him, at a distance of a hundred yards, he discovered a Rider galloping at a brisk trot, and something was familiar to her eyes when she discovered him bending over the horse's neck.

That figure, a little obese and squat, that rough outline, without grace, was that of Hamson's body, although now he was not wearing his imposing black frock coat, nor his branded vest, but a leather jacket, a cowboy hat and some blue trousers tucked into the bottom of his high leggings.

Mechanically, Frank backed his horse, taking better cover behind the trees until he let Hamson pass, and then, intrigued to see him go in such a direction, decided to follow him discreetly.

When he considered that he could not see him, he descended from the hill and put his horse at a trot, but he separated from the path and along a broken path, followed the same direction, until a quarter of an hour later, he managed to discover him galloping down the road. .

Half an hour later they were in sight of Thedford, and Frank guessed he would make his journey there.

The difficult thing was to follow him inside the town. Most likely he would find out, in which case his espionage plan would fail, but since there was no choice, he decided to take the chance.

Slowly he entered the village with his eyes fixed ahead, searching for Hamson's horse, but it must have seeped down some cross street, causing him to lose his track.

Annoyed, he decided to carry out an inspection throughout the center and walked through streets and alleys, until, when he came out into a spacious square, he discovered the banker's mount.

She was standing at the door of a two-story building, a beautiful modern brick construction, on the façade of which a sign announced:

«HOTEL TEXAS»

Frank prudently left his horse at the mouth of a nearby street and cautiously approached until he was in front of the hotel entrance. This was not only a modern and comfortable building, but the hotel was perhaps the most luxurious of all that side of the region.

The glass door turned on both sides, and behind a large and well decorated hall revealed the reception desk, as well as an elegant staircase that started at the bottom to slide in a spiral shape twisting to the right and left.

Through the windows, he discovered several hotel patrons, who by type claimed to be ranchers of excellent status, well-dressed dealers, and some individuals in exotic clothing, whom Frank quickly classified as professional gamblers.

What kind of hotel would this be, and what would Hamson have to do in it?

After a moment of hesitation, he made up his mind to penetrate. He would ask for a room and try to take advantage of this strange situation.

He walked over to the counter and requested a room to sleep. The clerk looked at him suspiciously for a moment, as if he did not judge him worthy of living in such an establishment, but he must have respected the colt that Frank was swinging negligently with his right hand, showing it to him more than as a curious object as a threat not to despise.

"It's three dollars," said the clerk.

Frank, without protesting the abuse, deposited the requested amount and the clerk asked:

" Your name? Do not shock him, it is an obligation to write it down in the entry book; otherwise, we are not curious.

"Billy Parker, is that okay?" Frank replied.

"Magnificent. Sign here.

And he offered him the book where he had just stamped Frank's patronymic imagination.

He glanced at the register, but did not discover Hamson's name on it.

"On the second floor, room number 20. Do you take a bath?

"Sometimes," replied Frank humorously. What other comforts can you offer me?

"You have a bar on the first floor and if you have a few dollars to spare, you have a recreation room.

"I love this hotel and I think I will stay longer. Although I am not dressed in full dress, do not think that I am undocumented. I came here precisely because a friend of mine from Nirvay recommended this hotel to me with great interest.

"From Nirvay?" Asked the clerk. I don't know, we have some clients there ...

"Sure. It was Mr. Hamson, the banker. I have an excellent account at your bank.

"Oh! He should have said it earlier ... Mr. Hamson ... Wait! I think better than room number 20, you will like room 32. It has a nice window overlooking the square.

"Thanks. Now I'm going to Nirvay. When I see Hamson, I will tell him that I was very well looked after.

The clerk gave a mischievous wink and replied in a low voice:

"Mr. Hamson is here. It has come a while ago.

"Devil, I love that! Where is he now?

"Chist ...! He's with the lady ...

"Ah! Already...! I should have suspected ...

"I don't know if he will stay. He had not come for a few days and the lady was already impatient.

"It's natural. Do you think it would be inappropriate to do to see him?

"I think so. He does not like to be seen. When he comes, he stays with the lady and they discuss the progress of the business. Then he leaves and never shows up in the gaming room.

"Understood. A man of his position cannot perform certain exhibitions ... It would not be serious ...

Sure, you understand. The hotel is very good, it is the best of Northwest Nebraska, but ... your enemies would accuse you of being part of a business where gambling is the main attraction. So if he hasn't told you about it, you better not see him.

"I think I will take your advice. Hamson is a good friend of mine and my father, but of course, his seriousness ... his daughter ... Tell me, where is he to run away from his path.

"The lady occupies the rooms at the back in the corridor to the right of the first floor.

"Thanks. I'm going to clean up a bit and then go down to the game room. There in Nirvay, it's disgusting, you can't play the spurs because they immediately criticize you.

"Well, here you can play up to the colt, don't worry.

Frank left a dollar on the table for the clerk, and satisfied with the collected reports, he headed for the stairs to ascend to the room that had been designated for him.

But when he reached the main floor, he glanced to convince himself that he was not seen and boldly advanced down the corridor, in the direction of the room, which, according to the clerk, belonged to "the lady."

Advancing on tiptoe, he reached the door, and indiscreetly leaned over, applying his right eye to the keyhole.

Through the small hole, he could only see a luxuriously dressed wooden bed and a small oval mirror dresser, the rest he could not distinguish for lack of visual space.

He could hear a rumor of conversation without being able to specify a word, which made him angry. He would have given up his fifty thousand dollars just to find out what they were talking about.

Something obscured for a moment the vision of the bed he was gazing at. It was a female silhouette that had stood in front of the keyhole.

Frank was able to admire a type of woman who was a little mature in age, but magnificently preserved. She was blonde, tall, slender, with morbid arms and fine, polished hands, on whose fingers several rings glittered. He had magnificent changeling greenish eyes and outrageously blond hair that had to be dyed.

From her outfit, she could only make out a sky-blue velvet jacket, with lace at the neck and the starting from the waist of a black skirt. He also admired a jeweled medallion that hung from her magnificent throat.

The lady was gesturing angrily and Frank looked away from the keyhole to apply his ear.

From her position, he was able to clearly grasp something she was saying:

"Sorry Wilfred, but things haven't been going well during this time. The hotel has a lot of spending and there were few customers and the few who came did not risk playing hard. This is very expensive as unfortunately you know and two strokes of fortune against our roulette have thrown me off balance again. I need that money without fail or I will have to close.

Frank waited. A mannish voice said something unintelligible and then, who was speaking, must have advanced because he could hear him say:

"I warned you, Martha you have cost me a lot and precisely the moment is very bad for me. You have to do whatever it takes and wait a few days. Precisely I came believing that you could leave me some money to solve a matter of great urgency ... It is well that it cannot be, but do not ask for a penny more for now. It can't be, I swear!

Frank looked back. He had seemed to hear footsteps and was venturing too far. He had recognized Hamson's voice, and with what he heard, he had enough to know what to expect.

He retraced his steps and descended into the hall.

The clerk was serving two new customers and did not see him leave.

Without wasting time he left the square, mounted his horse, and at a full gallop headed for Nirvay. He foresaw upcoming and decisive events and wanted to be prepared for them.

When he got to the town, he went directly to the sheriff's offices to give him an account of what he had discovered. Lang listened to him in amazement, and in a chaos of confusion, he asked:

"What do you deduce from all this, Frank?

"Isn't it clear? Hamson sustains at his expense that luxurious hotel and the whims and luxuries of its owner. Things are going badly and he's burying many thousands of dollars there. This clarifies why he has been forced to fake the theft of the fifty thousand dollars and it will not be this alone. She urges him for more money and I have threatened to ask for a review of accounts that could be the advance of his ruin. I will be very deceived if he does not try a new blow shortly, more desperate than the previous one.

"What can you try?

"I don't know, but you have to be vigilant, Lang. Do not forget that in Hamson's hands are the savings and small capital of many people, who would be plunged into ruin. I don't know how far the depositaries have evaded falling into it up to this point, but if we give it time to try another coup, the catastrophe will be certain.

"I don't imagine how we are going to be able to avoid it.

"Just keeping an eye on Hamson. Today I discovered your journey by chance, but just as you have tried that, I would try something else. Only you and I are in the secret and you and I must mount the surveillance dividing it to us. It will be hard work, but maybe not long.

"Well, I agree with your idea. As I must attend the offices during the day, you will be in charge of watching during that time, and at night I will make my rounds. I believe like you that Hamson has to try something decisive to solve this pothole and get out of it.

All right, Frank left the offices, an idea spinning in his head. It had occurred to him to rush events and he was going to do so immediately.

He spent the day discreetly prowling around Hamson's little house, hidden by overgrown depressions, and was severely tortured by twice discovering Sylvia in the small garden, one of them watering the plants and the other sitting in a garden. bench, reading a magazine.

The sight of the girl embittered his thoughts. He wondered what would become of her, when her father had to declare himself bankrupt, and worse still, what would happen if the proud banker committed some new and villainous action that brought him to the brink.

In other circumstances, he could have alleviated her pain and even looked after her future, but now, what could he try, if that incipient love that had united them years ago had died in her breast?

It was a torment for Frank to think of Sylvia and her future, but there was nothing he could do to prevent her ruin.

The well-being of many people in the town was in his hands and his duty dictated that he not sacrifice all of them just to save someone he owed nothing, but they were bad times and an anomalous and cruel situation.

When night came, he made out a horse that, making a detour so as not to enter the general path, was arriving at the little house. It was Hamson returning gloomy and in a hell of a mood.

Sylvia, concerned, wanted to probe his mood, but the banker was not up for confidences. He limited himself to saying that he had come from holding an interview with some of those who were preparing the great project he had in hand and that certain difficulties had arisen that he had to study to solve them.

And without even giving him footing to help calm his nerves by communicating the promise he had wrested from Frank, he locked himself in his office and had to give up seeing and talking to him for that day.

The next morning, Hamson showed up at the bank. His evening, which lasted late into the night, had been fruitful up to a point, for he had come to the conclusion of certain plans that he should not take long to implement.

There, he wrote a letter that he sent with one of his employees to Dennis's father's farm. It was a very studied letter, in which he requested a private loan of ten thousand dollars from him, with the promise of making the repayment eight days later.

He put as justification his commitment to pay the fifty thousand missing dollars on his own account and not counting that amount in cash at the time, he had to carry out negotiations for the sale of private securities, to collect said sum and enter it into the Bank's funds.

Hamson eagerly awaited the reply. Many things depended on the success of his letter that made him nervous and worried.

He was waiting for the answer, when something unexpected occurred that made him turn pale with anguish.

One of his employees had just presented him with a check for ten thousand dollars, an amount that Ted Neil, Frank's father, had deposited in the Bank and that the old merchant at the instigation of his son, claimed as cancellation of his checking account in the bank.

Hamson, furious, ordered that Frank be taken to his office, and when confronted with him, he exclaimed furiously:

"What is it you have proposed to yourself, Frank?"

"Simply collect money that my father has deposited here. You need it for an urgent business and since it is yours, I don't think anyone can deny you.

"Of course not, but ... this withdrawal from your checking account is very shocking. Have you set out to ruin the Bank?

"It is the same to me, but if that money was deposited here, it must be here and I don't think this constitutes a ruin.

"Possibly not, but you know how the Banks operate. Money is moved to produce and is not always in the cash box. Shares are bought, loans are made ...

"Yes, but you will not tell me that all the money is used, and if it is… give me its equivalent in easily salable and lossless securities. My father needs the money.

"Today precisely?

"Today precisely.

"Can't you wait two days? I have given an order to sell securities and have placed orders to cancel loans. I want to collect everything so that it is in the box, when you arrange for that humiliating inspection to be made.

"Sorry, but I can't wait. It must be today precisely.

Hamson was sweating like a damned man. He didn't want to get rid of a single dollar, and Frank's pretense was terribly upsetting all his plans.

Desperately, he struggled with Frank to get a two-day delay from him, but the uncompromising young man remained energetic in his claim. Not only did he not want to give the banker a break, but he was afraid that this money, all the product of many years of his father's work, would disappear with no possible way to rescue it.

The discussion was broken by the presence of one of the employees carrying a letter. It was the reply from Dennis's father.

Hamson, pulse trembling, tore the envelope open and peered inside, heaving a sigh of relief. Inside he had discovered several thousand dollar bills. Angrily, without asking permission, he eagerly read the contents of the letter. This was cold, though polite.

Rancher Powell told him that he answered her request more than to do her a personal favor, to help his neighbors to guarantee their interests, but there was nothing cordial between them after the incident that had caused such bitter troubles to his son, being the more lamentable the contemptuous attitude of Sylvia.

Hamson mentally cursed her daughter's decision to break up with Dennis, but nothing mattered to her now. This was a matter that belonged to the past, and the present showed facets that took him away from his projects millions of miles.

He raised his head and when he saw Frank's cold gaze he had an abscess of rage, and pulling out the bills, he threw them on the table roaring:

" Taking! And so this amount serves as poison to your father and to you! You have proposed to sink me, but you will not succeed. Hamson is stronger and smarter than all of you put together. There you have your money and one day you will regret this harassing attitude.

"Maybe, but ... I better want to regret that, than having allowed my father to lose his savings.

Hamson, fierce, got up screaming:

"Get out of here, aggressive gunman! You use your skill in handling the revolver and my years to threaten me. Your money! Do you think I was going to stay with him?

"I can no longer believe it, since it has been restored to me. It is more in reparation, I will hasten to communicate the news to those who await the result of this management. I will tell them that you are a serious and solvent man, that you honor your commitments and that they can proceed to withdraw their deposits, sure that they will not oppose such a legitimate right.

And with a comic greeting he left the office.

Hamson stiffened at the threat. If he complied with it, and depositaries began to flow to the window, only the contents of his revolver, well applied to his head, could solve the situation.

And fearful of having to resort to such a measure, he hastened to order his employees to warn whoever came in search of money, that he had left and that they would not be able to withdraw funds until the next day. It was the only thing he could do to buy time, the time that was crushing him.

CHAPTER X

CORRELATED

Hamson had counted not only on stopping the coup until the next day, but until the following day, since the following was Sunday, and being a holiday, no one could force him to break the precepts by opening the offices. He had almost two days of respite; Two days that, well used, could be very useful to him and he devoted all his energy to using them.

At one o'clock, he ordered his employees to leave work. Only one farmer had come forward for fifty dollars, and Hamson had been quick to order that it be paid, for the sum was not worthy of alarm.

When he was left alone, he closed inside the Bank and feverishly began to check a cash count in the boxes. He needed every last penny and the last pledgeable value and he was not planning to leave anything but the walls of the bank and the papers of a future useless job.

When he had everything together, he carefully packed it in a large leather sack and locked it in his office. Hamson was decomposed and enraged at Frank, who had materially sunk him, frustrating a great project he had, to have saved from his account not only those missing first fifty thousand dollars, but another similar amount.

Now he could no longer rely on tricks. He was harassed and on the verge of being discovered and had to take advantage of the few hours of freedom he had left to flee with the poor crumbs he had left.

He could no longer count on the ten thousand dollars he had so treacherously taken from Powell. That demon Frank, whom he would have liked to get rid of before escaping, had been smarter than all, guessing at his financial situation and no longer cared what happened, but what might happen. If Frank's suspicion went any further, perhaps even running away could not be of any use to him.

But he had to try. His situation was frankly distressing. This woman from Thedford had led him in a fast and agonizing way to the edge of the precipice, and what he regretted the most was that this sacrifice was not going to serve him even to preserve her, because now he would be forced to flee very far to avoid that the claws of the Law provided him with an indefinite accommodation, very antagonistic to the one he had enjoyed until then.

For a moment, the sight of his daughter disturbed him. He couldn't take her with him, for she would be a hindrance and a danger; Nor could he give her an account of her situation that there was no way to justify more than by revealing the truth, which she resisted due to a trace of modesty, and she had to leave her to her will without means of fortune and only with that small farm that neither even she could save her when it comes to liquidating bankruptcy.

But the self-preservation instinct was stronger than any other feeling. Either way, fleeing or staying, Sylvia's situation would be the same, and he, on the other hand, would not enjoy the possibility of saving himself.

Fate had arranged it that way and that is how he had to accept it whether he regretted it or not.

When there was no money left to collect, he did a review of books and papers and chose the most compromising ones, as well as proof of current accounts. He left nothing of value behind him but it was the building, but if with their value they intended to wipe the deficit on a pro rata basis, he would leave behind a schism since no one could justify what he had deposited.

In the middle of the afternoon, he left the Bank from its back, taking care before not being seen. It was the hour when the ranch laborers would begin to flock to the town and he did not want to be seen by them.

Fortunately, the back of the Bank overlooked a little-frequented alley, and choosing others as lonely as her, she reached the outskirts and headed for her farm.

Once there, he entered the shed where he kept his buggy and hid the leather jacket under the seat. Later he collected some objects and papers in his office that he did not want to fall into the hands of the sheriff and went to the living room, where Sylvia was embroidering in very dark thoughts.

The banker, showing great joy, approached her, and after kissing her, said:

"Listen Sylvia, I'm about to finish a great deal. You know I hinted at something about him; Well, I'm going to tell you what it is about, so that you realize its magnitude and help me with a small need that requires your cooperation. Colossal works will soon begin to take advantage of the waters of the Missouri and create an irrigation zone for the entire valley, a new railroad branch that will make that old Missouri stagecoach line disappear, and a power plant that will give fluid and power. to the region.

«The project is great, but the competitors who want to beat us by the hand are behind it. Someone has suspected that I am an important agent in the project and they monitor me so that, for my knowledge, I can reach the large capitalists who finance the works and today precisely, I have to leave here to hold the last and final interview with them, but I suspect that someone is after me to find out who it is and hinder the project for their benefit.

"That's why I need your help to march and mislead whoever wants to spy on me.

"Okay dad, but what can I do?

"I'm gonna tell you. You are going to ride in the gig to which you will hook two good horses and as if you were going for a ride, you take it to the forest three miles from here, near the river. You know where it is, because we have had a snack some afternoons, together in it.

«Hitch one more horse in front of you and when you are in the forest, you unlock it, hide the gig and return mounted on horseback. If someone sees you leaving and then returning without the gig, you say that a wheel has broken and that you are looking for me.

"That is a very common accident that people will believe. When you have returned, you and I will go out on horseback as if we were going in search of the damaged carriage. When we see us together on horseback, no one will suspect that I am going out with the intention of going on a trip and they will not worry about us.

«When we reach the gig, I will leave with him and you will return a while later with your horse and mine, then, if someone asks you, you say that I have arranged to fix the gig and you lock yourself in the farm.

"Very good, dad; I will, but where are you going? You never tell me anything.

"This time I'll tell you, silly. I'm going to Rita Park.

"Are you going to be away for a long time?

"Not. I think I will be here first thing on Monday to open the Bank. Don't worry and hurry up.

The young woman obeyed, and going down to the shed, she hitched up the three horses and left for the indicated place, ready to carry out her father's instructions to the letter.

Frank, who, ambushed in his observatory, did not lose sight of the little house, saw Sylvia leave with the buggy in which he did not discover anyone and wondered where she would go. But since she made trips to the village in the carriage and sometimes took it out to ride the horses, he was not alarmed.

Only the impulse to go out to meet her to accompany her overpowered him, but his duty to watch over Hamson, whom he distrusted more and more, stopped him.

Three-quarters of an hour later, he discovered a rider returning to the cottage, and his keen eyes recognized Sylvia, which alarmed him, for he was returning without the buggy.

An unstoppable impulse forced him to leave his observatory, and making a detour to border the sensation of espionage, he went out to meet Sylvia.

She made a gesture of displeasure, but quickly regretted it, and lowering her head, she tried to move on.

Frank passed his horse asking:

"Sylvia, how are you doing at this hour, alone around here? It's night and ...

"Is it someone's account? I went out for a buggy ride and a wheel broke about two miles from here. I come looking for my father to accompany me to fix it.

"What are you going to bother him for? A banker with a belly and polished hands cannot stoop to such duties. I can...

"Thanks. It's our account and my father hasn't forgotten that he was a rancher, believe it or not.

"Okay, I see you dislike favors you don't ask for. As for the others ...

"It is the same to me. I'm sorry I asked you for none and I relieve you of fulfilling it. I haven't even told my father because I know he would reject it.

"Okay, despite that I am not going to do it. The word of a man is word.

"Thanks… sorry, but I'm in a hurry.

And spurring the horse, he trotted toward the cottage.

Frank was not surprised by the mishap. A wheel bucks easily, but he was curious if Hamson would be able to come in person to fix the carriage.

When he lost sight of Sylvia, he returned to his hiding place. He would see if the banker was dating his daughter and then wait for Lang. Night was upon us and the sheriff had to replace him.

It didn't take long to see that Sylvia had told him the truth. Shortly afterwards the young woman and the banker, both on horseback, crossed in the soft evening twilight before Frank's sharp gaze.

He did not observe anything in particular in the rancher. He wore a leather jacket and gray trousers with high boots and carried a sack over his horse's neck that should contain tools for grooming.

Frank didn't want to move from his observatory. Following them was very exposed, because the way was open and after having already seen Sylvia, it would be suspicious to show himself again in their eyes.

Half an hour later Lang showed up, and Frank realized what had happened.

"Do you suspect something, Frank?" Asked the sheriff.

"Not really. I saw her go out with the buggy and come back without it. Now the two have gone on horseback. I don't think Hamson will try anything with his daughter as a drag. It may be an unforeseen incident. I don't think it will take us long to check it out.

"Well, if you want, you can go.

"Not. I will wait until they return. I don't want to leave you alone without that assurance.

The wait was long. The accident had to be serious or Hamson's ability very little and Frank was beginning to get impatient with a slight doubt.

"If you take a quarter of an hour more, I will try to locate you, I am not sure now that all this is a natural thing.

Lang hinted:

"If Hamson suspects that he is being watched, he may not be.

"That's what I don't know for sure, but just in case, I won't let him take initiatives. He is smart and a desperate man like him must be attentive to all contingencies.

Ten minutes later they caught the trot of horses and hiding in the woods, Frank said:

"There they return, but ... it seems to me that they return without the gig. Perhaps they have had to give up the arrangement.

More when in the light of the moon that began to appear clear and round on the plain they discovered the two horses and only Sylvia on one of them, Frank emitted a curse.

" Ray! This does not smell good to me, Lang ... She with the two horses, Hamson does not return nor the buggy either. Was it useful to start the escape?

"You have to find out, Frank. If we are careless and let him reach the divide, we can say goodbye to reaching out to him.

Frank did not wait any longer, and throwing his horse over the hedge, he went out to meet the young woman.

Angrily, she stopped the horse's trot and shouted:

"Are you spying on me, Frank? It is very suspicious that ...

"Suspect what you want, it's the same to me. Where's your father?

"Fixing the gig.

" Where?

" What do you care? Anywhere.

Frank angrily shook her by the arm, roaring:

" Stupid! You are playing the game of the greatest villainy he has ever committed in his life and he has committed many. You are helping him to flee forever from you and the town.

"Lie!" She roared indignantly. " I know where it is going and where it is! You are a villain.

"And you an obtuse one. Your father is bankrupt, he has misappropriated the funds of the Bank, he has faked a theft of a bag with fifty thousand dollars that he had not deposited in it, as we will demonstrate in his day and how he is led to have to account for that money that is It has been eaten by a cheerful woman from Thedford, as I will also show you, run away.

«Your father is a villain who not only ruined himself and he has ruined you, but he has stolen from the whole town and he and no one but him was the one who robbed the stage and killed Jasper to recover the sack containing lead, and pretend that its contents had been stolen.

Sylvia could not resist the terrible blow that those energetic accusations meant to her, and with a cry of agony, she bent over the horse's neck and rolled on the ground, where she was lifeless.

Frank rushed to his aid, and Lang, furious, yelled:

"Good you have done it! You have given him a death blow and now we cannot know where that toad has gone.

"But we will find him, Lang. We will find him, even if he goes to hell itself. A gig does not gallop what two horses like ours. Help me. We are going to leave this idiot on his farm and we are going to go after that pig's tracks. He's been very smart, but he hasn't had Frank Neil.

Frank mounted his horse and Lang lifted Sylvia's body, handing it to her to place in front of him. Then he jumped into the saddle of his saddle and taking charge of the two horses, they trotted to the little house, which was not far away.

Frank pounded on the fence gate, and shortly thereafter the gardener appeared. Frank, without dismounting, exclaimed:

"Please take care of the lady. He has fainted while returning and has fallen off his horse. I think it will not be a matter of care, but it was convenient that they lay her down and go in search of the village doctor. I'm sure you will need it.

He handed over the girl's body, left the two horses locked to the door, and facing Lang, said:

" Go?

"Good, but wait for me to stop by the offices first. The chase can be long and difficult and we are not prepared for it. It is better to lose a quarter of an hour more than to have to give up completely later.

At a demonic trot they headed into town, stopping before the offices. Lang prevented himself from ammunition, another revolver, and the rifle, supplied his partner with projectiles, and put some preserves in a sack. He also took two canteens of water and two blankets.

"Come on, Frank" he said "now we can gallop to the divide without stopping for lack of precautions.

At random they took the path that Sylvia had brought back. They did not know which way they had headed, but instinct warned them that the shortest and safest path for Hamson was the dividing line.

CHAPTER XI

THE CATASTROPHE

It was already night and the darkness was not a good ally to be able to quickly locate the banker's footprints. A soft bluish moonlight faintly illuminated the landscape and its glow was too dim to be able to register the terrain.

They had to trust a bit at random. At the moment the road was that of the North, but no one; he knew where he might have drifted to turn, either toward the Missouri or toward the Lupp, in order to throw off all pursuit.

The first obstacle that presented itself before them was the small forest where Sylvia hid the gig to return in search of her father. Frank did not believe that it was hidden in him, but wanted to take a look before continuing, and stopping the horse, he dismounted.

Shortly after entering, among the trees he discovered something that he considered a good clue. Hamson had left the small sack of tools that he had taken from the farm to justify his departure.

With this detail, the young man searched the floor attentively and soon discovered the tracks of the wheels of the buggy marking its taxiing towards the West.

"Go ahead!" He said to the sheriff. Hamson must continue towards the general path "and he told him what he had discovered.

When they were cutting ground to reach the path, a distant tinkle reached their ears and from the top where they were walking, they discovered the white lights of two movable lanterns.

"That's where the Missouri stage goes!" Lang warned.

"He was leaving the town when we.

The heavy hulk was ahead of them and they were soon out of sight.

"Do you think he will dare to follow the general path?" Asked the sheriff.

"I suspect not. You don't want to be seen. If you follow that same direction, you will try to do it through inconspicuous places and we will try to follow a similar path.

Through meadows and fields, sometimes crossing rough terrain, they followed ahead without discovering a trace. Although they galloped steadily, they had failed to catch up with the fugitive.

Frank was feeling nervous. He feared that he had gotten lost and knew that a mistake was to give Hamson the possibility of filtering through one of the two divisions.

They had been about five miles when Lang pointed to a hedge, saying:

"I see a strange lump there, Frank. It is something that sticks out of the bushes.

They drifted toward him and as they approached, Frank swore an oath. Hidden in the hedge, the abandoned buggy appeared. The horses were not there, but the carriage was.

"It could not have gone very far," assured the young man. Those horses are not good for long races.

He scanned the terrain again, and his keen eyesight found hoof tracks heading for the road.

"Come on," he said, "he must have tried to cross to the other side. Towards Missouri.

They galloped on, but before reaching the path, they discovered a lone horse browsing in the grass.

"This is one of his horses," said Frank. Where is the other one?

"Between her legs," Lang assured. He was not going to leave on foot.

"Of course not, but ... I'm not convinced. With that penco he cannot even get to Seneca, how much more to the border.

Suddenly he slapped his forehead and roared:

"Gallop Lang! We have to achieve stagecoach.

" Because?

"You don't suspect it? Hamson is smart as hell. He had to step out of the stage to ride it. He will calculate that while we are wasting time searching for him in the carriage or on the horses, the stagecoach will have taken him two hours from the divide. Come on, Lang!

And at full gallop they ran down the path, on their way to the next town.

★ ★ ★

Frank's suspicions were not unfounded. Hamson had calculated everything to the minute and was sure of succeeding in this posthumous and desperate endeavor.

On the road, posted, he waited for the vehicle to pass and made it stop.

He claimed that he had received an urgent notice to go to Marsland and by shortcuts he had managed to reach the vehicle without time to wait for the one that two days later would cross the town.

He got on the box with the mayoral, to whom he gave a good tip and told him his story. He had to deposit in the aforementioned town an important and scaled amount of what had happened in the previous one, he wanted to guard it in person.

The mayoral, little aware of what had happened in Nirvay, did not suspect anything extraordinary and agreed to allow the banker to ride with him on the box.

Hamson, relieved of the anguish that overwhelmed him, placed the sack between his legs and made sure that the revolver easily slid out of its holster.

He was ready to defend himself until the last moment, although he was almost certain that his maneuver would mislead his enemies and that when they wanted to realize his escape, he would be far from Nebraska.

About nine o'clock they reached Seneca, where the team of horses had to be changed and the travelers would have an hour to dine in the canteen of the Casa de Postas.

Hamson refused to descend. He had eaten and had no appetite at all, and so, while the overseer and the travelers alighted to regain strength, he remained at the top of the box, guarding his sack and staring at his back so as not to be surprised.

The grooms changed the horses, leaving the vehicle ready for departure, and when half an hour had not elapsed since their arrival, Hamson suffered a terrible start.

He heard the clatter of the gallop of some horses advancing along the path he had left behind, and turning angrily, he glanced over.

Soon after, he issued a terrible oath. He had recognized the horses and with them Lang and Frank.

There was no longer any doubt that he had been discovered and like a cornered bear he looked everywhere.

He had only one chance to flee and he did not disdain it. He grasped the bridles of the four draft horses within reach of his hands and, cracking the whip, he forced the animals to start quickly.

The vehicle, like an exhalation, tumbling terribly, slid down the dusty path, and the roar of its march and the mad jingle of the bells, alarmed the overseer, who, leaving the table, went like a whirlwind to the door, shouting:

"The horses are escaping, they are escaping!

At that moment Lang and Frank stopped their sweaty mounts at the door of the Post Office, and Frank, facing the frightened foreman, asked:

" What's going on?

"The devil who knows ... The carriage stood there while we had dinner and suddenly it started ...

" Only?

"Yes ... that is, no ... Mr. Hamson from Nirvay was on the box ... he's going to ...

Frank didn't let him finish; he propelled his horse forward, shouting:

"Lang, gallop, that's ours!

And leaving the mayoral even more surprised, they disappeared into a cloud of dust in pursuit of the stagecoach.

It was lost in the distance like a ghost in the dust, but Frank and Lang trusted their horses and were sure to catch up with it.

A terrible struggle was established between the vehicle and the brave mounts. Hamson, madly, whipped them mercilessly, forcing them to give their maximum performance, and from time to time he turned his head in anguish, realizing with terror that instead of blowing up the wind he was losing ground.

Mad with rage, he abandoned the reins and drew his revolver. Before letting himself be caught, he would die with weapons in hand and try to drive his enemies away.

Blindly shot. The projectile whistled past Lang and Frank, and Frank rushed to reply, firing at the carriage.

Hamson no longer cared about driving the vehicle. With his chest resting on the edge of the upper part and sticking his head out, he fired fiercely at both riders and they replicated his shots trying to reach him.

The car, without direction, was like a meteor rolling at random. A huge pothole made him wobble, being about to throw the banker out of him, but he desperately clung to the top and managed to keep his balance, but he could not prevent the leather sack with the product of his robbery, was thrown out on the road.

Out of his mind, he watched helplessly as Lang paused to pick it up, then struggled to join his partner in continuing the tragic pursuit.

And so, in this contest, devouring terrain, the vehicle continued its fantastic race, now through rough and dangerous terrain and the two riders, tough and obstinate, followed after the stagecoach ready to burst their mounts rather than give up hunting.

Suddenly an unexpected catastrophe occurred. The heavy hulk, flying faster than rolling down the open path at the edge of an embankment, got out of the way. One of the wheels on the left side snapped off its axle when it stumbled on a cliff and the vehicle leaned towards that side, remaining for a moment in an unstable attitude, until under its own weight it sank into the void, dragging behind it to the horses and the crazy Hamson.

When Lang and Frank, livid with surprise, were able to restrain their mounts and look over the cliff, they had nothing to do. The carriage lay at the bottom more than twenty meters high, completely shattered.

$$\star\ \star\ \star$$

The sun was high enough when Lang and Frank, with the traces of the terrible day on their faces, entered Nirvay, heading straight for Hamson's estate.

They were going to give Sylvia the terrible news, and Frank, seized with an unstoppable anxiety, was devastated when he pondered the situation in which the young woman remained.

This, pale and nervous, received them, trying to appear serenity and asked trembling:

"May I know what brings you to this house?

Frank, visibly moved, exclaimed:

"Sylvia, I am sorry to have terrible news for you, but there is no use hiding it from you. Your father is dead.

She gave a terrible scream, and clutching his jacket, moaned:

"Frank! You ... you have killed him!

"No, Sylvia. He would not have been able to do it, not for him, but for you ... His folly, his ambition and his madness have killed him; listen and you will know many things that you ignore.

And succinctly he gave an account of everything without omitting any detail.

She listened to him between sobs of infinite anguish, and when Frank finished the story, she cried:

"Oh my God, what a shame! My father a ...

"Listen, Sylvia" Frank interrupted "if you want, no one has a need to know. We can say that he died in an accident. While he waited at the Post Office, the horses ran wild and threw him over the cliff. Lang is willing to endorse this white lie ... for you and me.

"Why you, Frank? My father has been your enemy and he has done you a lot of damage. Now I realize it.

"It is true, but he has already paid for his faults and you have nothing to do with them.

"But I have done wrong with you, Frank. I was influenced by his words and advice and believed ... My God, I will never forgive myself!

"But I do forgive you, Sylvia. I have to, because despite everything ... I still love you like then or maybe more. I came only with the hope of being able to rescue your love and I still do not despair of it.

"And you, would you be able to join ... the daughter of a scammer?

"What does it matter to me what he could be, if you are not?

"Oh, Frank, you are very good, so much… so, that I feel ashamed to hear you… I… I… loved you, I still loved you despite Dennis… but my father…

"Forget that, Sylvia. If it is true that you still love me like then, everything can be fixed.

" How? My father has squandered the bank's money. He is bankrupt and that cannot be hidden …

"I think so. Sylvia. Here, in this bag, we have saved part of what was taken, I withdrew ten thousand dollars yesterday from my father, which I can have, but I also have fifty thousand of my own, with them we can face the situation, open the Bank, attend to the most peremptory and study how to reorganize its operation. I am willing to work like a beast to get the business afloat. I never dreamed of managing a bank, but I consider myself suitable for it.

"But…

"Do not object. You are the only heir to your father. If we marry, I, as your husband, must attend to the business. We will get you afloat, we will strengthen the confidence of the neighbors and we will be happy. Time is a sedative for pain and a good sponge to erase facts that the wind takes away little by little. Do you have something to object to?

"Nothing, Frank, except that I consider myself unworthy of that affection and that sacrifice that you try for me. I was a frivolous woman who allowed myself to be seduced by the mirage of grandeur and pageantry, and now reality puts the terrible truth before my eyes.

"Good, but that can also be erased. Forget that you went to a school like that and look back on the happy days when you were the daughter of a rancher and I was a peon on your ranch. So we go back to living that life, which is ours, the true West, the rest can be left behind like a dream.

She threw herself into his arms, sobbing:

"Thank you Frank, I want it to be that way. May that be forgotten as a terrible dream and may this happiness that you bring me and that I do not think I deserve be not a dream.

END